Dr Ian Marsh has been a university lecturer for many years and has taught, researched and written widely on crime and criminal justice. He is the author of numerous academic books on crime and justice and this is his second fictional book – following on from *Murderer: On Your Mark*, published by Austin Macauley in December 2015.

'Ian Marsh has used his experience to create a worthy academic crime novel, featuring a narrator who definitely doesn't put his students first. Murderer on Your Mark is a wicked poison pill of a debut.' Paul Johnston, CWA Dagger Winner

Ian Marsh

GEMMA MAKES HER MARK

To Alison

Thanks

Ian 2018

AUSTIN MACAULEY PUBLISHERS™

LONDON • CAMBRIDGE • NEW YORK • SHARJAH

A CIP catalogue record for this title is available from the British Library.

This is a fictional story and therefore any resemblance to actual persons, living or dead, or particular institutions or actual events is purely coincidental.

ISBN 9781787105768 (Paperback)
ISBN 9781787105775 (E-Book)

www.austinmacauley.com

First Published (2017)
Austin Macauley Publishers™ Ltd.
25 Canada Square
Canary Wharf
London
E14 5LQ

Acknowledgements

In trying to capture the feel and detail of the period and places that this story is set in, I am indebted to many people who invariably have answered my calls with such willingness and patience. I would like to thank, in particular, Lena Simic and her Aunt, Branka Franicevic, for sharing with me their knowledge of the people and history of Dubrovnik.

As ever, the team at Austin Macauley, and particularly Walter Stephenson and Vinh Tran, have helped enormously in turning my script into a finished product.

Finally and most importantly, thanks to Gaynor for her continued support and flow of ideas.

PART ONE: FRIDAY 24 JULY – SATURDAY 25 JULY 1981

Mark was starting to get a barbecue going in the back garden of the end terrace cottage he and Gemma had bought a few months previously. She'd be back from a court visit shortly – having tried, no doubt, to make the case for a probation order rather than a prison sentence on behalf of one of her hapless regulars – and he'd promised her they'd make the most of the still light, mid-July summer evenings. Having tried paper and twigs, he was already onto the firelighters but with little luck so far. He pondered that perhaps it represented something of an allegory for his recent life – it had been difficult to get things started since his release on parole the previous winter, after just over six years in prison.

They had decided on Petworth as a suitable place to start their life together, between Littlehampton, home to the probation office that Gemma was based at, and Farnham, where her mother rattled around in the large mock Tudor house she'd been left with after Gemma's father died. Mark had used some of the money he had saved from the wreckage of his marriage to Fiona, and which he'd had no need or chance to use while in prison, for the deposit and Gemma had arranged a small mortgage – £25,000 wasn't a bad price and it was a lovely area and a nice place to live. However in spite of that, and even after just a few months, Mark couldn't throw off a general and growing feeling of dissatisfaction, or maybe more accurately of boredom, with his situation.

The market town of Petworth itself was picture-postcard quaint: cobbled streets around the centre, and home to a growing number of antique shops, reflecting its rapidly developing reputation as a centre for the trade. The imposing Petworth House was the major – really, only – tourist attraction; it dominated the town but Mark knew little of its history, apart from the fact that prior to being handed over to the National Trust shortly after the Second World War it had belonged to various aristocratic families. He was more familiar with the little stone cross in the local cemetery commemorating the 32 boys and masters who'd been killed when Petworth Boys Schools was hit, supposedly mistakenly, by German bombs in 1942. Apparently the bombs had been aimed at Petworth House itself, which presumably and according to local gossip was being used at the time for military purposes of some sort.

Things hadn't happened for Mark as he'd envisioned when he was counting time and making plans at Ford Open Prison, just down the road from Littlehampton. Completing his sentence there explained his contact with the probation office in Littlehampton and with Gemma in particular. He had tried his hand at this and that, but nothing had taken off. Most recently, and trying to benefit from the growing antique market, he had been buying and selling bits and pieces of antique furniture. He'd immersed himself in recent copies of the renowned *Miller's Guides to Antiques and Collectables* and idled away a good few hours, merging into days, following up local ads and pottering around at auction viewings and sales. He fancied he had become something of an amateur expert and had even managed to sell a couple of nursing chairs and a Victorian rosewood wheel barometer at a recent furniture sale, but really that had only just covered the commission he ended up being charged. Nonetheless it had been reasonably pleasant inveigling his way into the local antique scene, and the chance of making a real find and potential profit added some interest and even excitement to the whole endeavour. At the same time as dabbling in the trade he'd made a few acquaintances at sales run by Weller's, who had recently expanded from running just agricultural and livestock auctions. Their morning sales invariably led to a few of the regular buyers and dealers heading for a liquid lunch at the Angel Inn in the centre of town. Mark was a good deal younger than them, most of whom looked well past fifty; he hadn't changed his style of dress from pre-prison days and liked to think his Wrangler shirt, Levi's, brown leather jacket and cowboy-style boots set him apart from the Barbour jackets and check shirts favoured by the professional antique dealers. To be fair, though, they were a relatively interesting bunch and Mark had enjoyed these almost weekly events, even if the tales of bargains and profits became more and more incredible as the afternoons wore on. The thing was, it just wasn't enough or what he wanted; he knew it was basically a distraction, one which Gemma was becoming increasingly irritated by. Even though Gemma had been understanding up to a point about the difficulties he would inevitably face after a lengthy spell in prison, her snide comments and digs about her bringing in all the money had become gradually more frequent. It was a little unfair; after all, the problems faced by ex-cons was something she was more than familiar with, given her own job. He'd kept on top of the domestic jobs, the shopping and cooking and cleaning, but she always managed to point out something that hadn't been done in the appropriate time or manner.

***

Mark was only thirty-three: just over ten years ago his life had seemed to be mapped out, and in retrospect in a far from unpleasant manner. He'd got a lecturing position in the Sociology Department at Sussex University after completing his Masters' degree at Kent and within a year or so was beginning to be seen as something of a rising star in the discipline. He'd published a few papers in respected, subject-specialist journals and even been paid a reasonable publisher's advance for editing a collection of classic social theory extracts deemed suitable for undergraduate students. He had been well liked in the department and popular with the students too; he'd always had a sort of naturally outgoing streak which enabled him to mix with the older members of the Sociology department as well as the more trendy, newer staff and post-graduates.

Mark opened a can of Foster's lager. It had been over eight months since his release, after serving just under six years of his life sentence for murder. On the face of it that had been quite a result. He was fortunate that there had been a general shift towards emphasising the rehabilitation of prisoners in the early 1970s and he had made sure that he played the part of the model prisoner – not overly sycophantic but not too arrogant or difficult to manage either. He had succeeded in convincing everyone, including most critically the Parole Board, that he was a reformed character and certainly no danger to the wider public. It hadn't taken him long to realise that the key indicators needed to get an early parole date were to demonstrate genuine remorse and to satisfy the experts that the crimes themselves were clearly out of character, driven by a kind of temporary loss of control, and therefore would never be repeated. Although his crimes had certainly attracted a good deal of publicity at the time they had faded from the general consciousness since then. Even Mark found it somewhat difficult to believe that he had convinced Jean, his mother-in-law, that he actually found her attractive, while at the same time slowly filling her with a mixture of illegal drugs and natural poisons. And after she had passed away without any suspicion resting on him, a similar strategy had worked on his father-in-law, Gordon. That might not have involved part-way seducing him, as he had done with Jean, but the fact that his father-in-law had pretty much given up on things, including his health, after Jean's death made it that much easier. Nonetheless, Mark hadn't been able to help the same thought coming back to him time and again during his prison sentence: if it hadn't been for Justine's bloody self-righteous indignation, if she'd supported him, then he – in fact, they – would have got away with it.

Of course, the parole requirements meant that he would be on 'licence', as they put it, for the rest of his sentence, and subject to recall should he offend again, but he had no intention of that – or no intention of ever being caught and recalled, at least. Initially Gemma had been his probation contact and support during the final stages of his sentence and the pre-parole period. She had accompanied the senior probation officer and her boss, David, on his initial visits to supervise Mark after he'd been transferred to Ford Open Prison, and then taken him on herself after David's surprise early retirement. Gemma was young, twenty-three, when he first encountered her, and just a few months into her first job since graduating, typically (and a little ironically) with a degree in Sociology. He liked the way she wore close fitting clothes that highlighted her figure, the pencil skirts and tight designer jeans in particular. To begin with, he hadn't been able to work out whether she was really posh or just radiated it. He had soon realised there was no pretence.

After years of celibacy and without any recent practice, Mark had enjoyed charming and intriguing her and she had seemed to like the attention too. Sure enough, soon after his release they had become an item and then moved in together. They had played it by the book and had come clean about their relationship; and so as to avoid any conflict of interest, the official supervision of his rehabilitation had been passed on to one of Gemma's colleagues, Mathew. A somewhat more typical example of the probation officer role than Gemma, or to put it more accurately an absolute stereotype of it, Mathew was a slightly earnest, bearded ex-hippy type who enjoyed the opportunity to have an articulate client with whom he could discuss music, film and any other examples of cultural coolness that he could engineer into their conversations. Mark found Mathew's snobbish take on any and all of those topics profoundly irritating, but he had always been a good manager of other's impressions of him and was happy to play along with things. After he had lent Mathew a couple of his Balzac novels there was no looking back. Mathew was convinced they had made some kind of intellectual contact with one another and Mark had no reason to disabuse him; he was well aware of the sense in keeping his parole supervisor on side.

Thinking back, Mark realised how easy it was to forget unpleasant things; as with most ex-cons he'd vowed never to go back, but by contrast with them, he liked to think he meant it. When Gemma had met him at the prison gates on his release last November, Mark had been convinced that he would just enjoy whatever life threw at him and that anything would be better than the last few years. He wouldn't care what he had to do or what he had or didn't have, he would relish just being away from the petty constraints of institutional life. However, and as he was well aware from having come across studies on the recidivism of offenders when teaching the sociology of deviance in his previous existence, the memories receded pretty quickly; really, when he took the time to reflect, his personality hadn't changed that much after all. Maybe the personality he had used to convince the Parole Board had, but not the real one.

Post-prison, things had started quite nicely. Gemma had kept her job and he'd settled into the flat above a florist's in a small parade of shops just out of the centre of Littlehampton; it was not far from Gemma's apartment, close to the station and overlooking the river Arun. In fact, going well over and above the usual post-release support offered by the probation service, and presumably without their knowledge, Gemma had found and arranged the renting of the flat for him before his release. Mark had given her access to his share of the divorce settlement, which considering his status as a convicted criminal hadn't been too bad. Somewhat paradoxically, the murder of her parents had left his ex-wife a very wealthy woman and she hadn't objected to Mark's solicitor sorting out a reasonable deal from the sale of the house they'd bought together; no doubt she'd just been glad to see the back of him and to move on with her life.

The first few months and over the Christmas and New Year had been pretty good. Gemma and he had not been a couple immediately, although Mark assumed that they both thought that was inevitable. From their first meeting at Ford Open Prison, the atmosphere and rapport between them, along with the comments and looks they gave one another, had convinced him they had a future. After his release, it had been Mark's intention to play it reasonably cool to begin with, and certainly not to appear too desperate. He had made it clear that he wanted to keep in touch with Gemma and was pretty sure she felt the same – after all, she had helped arrange the flat for him and taken the trouble to collect him from Ford on his release date. As well as that, she had persuaded her new boss to let her continue with his supervision immediately after release, fortunately a practice that was being encouraged as offering some kind of continuity of support and aid to rehabilitation for ex-prisoners.

In the early days of his life on the outside again they had met regularly for coffee and for what were presumably and officially supposed to be 'post-release support meetings'; but which went well beyond the required time or usual locations and soon involved them talking and drinking until throwing out time. Mark had even encouraged Gemma to go on a couple of dates with a friend of one of her friends. It might have been taking playing it cool a bit far but his idea had been to act as a kind of sophisticated mentor to her and pretend to help her find a suitable boyfriend, while at the same time letting her see how much more interesting and challenging a prospect he would be. He assumed it had all worked pretty much according to plan when one of their increasingly regular late-night heart to hearts, with him offering her the wisdom of his knowledge of the male species, had led to a hug, and then her letting him slip his hand under her dress. It seemed to Mark that was what they had both been waiting for; he had spent that night at Gemma's flat. While it had been a few years since he had been touched by anyone apart from himself, there was certainly something special about the way she controlled him while seemingly abandoning herself. She certainly knew how to enjoy herself.

It never crossed Mark's mind that the managing of it all might well have been the other way around; he always assumed that no one could be as manipulative as he was. He had never doubted his attractiveness to women, and even Justine's abandonment of him and the subsequent events hadn't undermined his self-confidence that much. On occasion he had found himself wondering if his tendency to believe in his own superiority had been the cause of his problems, but he never allowed such doubts to take root.

***

Gemma had been quite a catch and Mark had revelled in the excitement and freedom she offered him after years away. After the initial pretence of their official, ex-con and probation officer, relationship, their meetings soon turned into nights out, eating and drinking; and she had certainly proved to be more than the naïve do-gooder that had been his first impression when she had visited him at Ford as a newly qualified probation officer. Mark had soon discovered that she had family money behind her and that her job, while not just posturing, was also and clearly not the vocation he had initially assumed it was for her. There was more to it than that, though. There was a confidence about her he hadn't noticed straight away; it was apparent in the way she dressed and the way she was when they first made love. Of course, things had moved on since the mid-1970s, and maybe the 1980s would prove to be different, but nonetheless she dressed differently to his previous girlfriends – classy dresses and smart suits which had a timeless air to them rather than the ex-hippy stuff which he'd been used to. Not yet twenty-five years old, Gemma could make herself look either younger or older depending on the context, and with a natural elegance she always managed to look taller than her five foot five. She had fine auburn hair, olive green eyes and a full figure – 'voluptuous' might be over-stating it, but she reminded him of Hollywood actresses of the 1930s and '40s, Jean Harlow, Veronica Lake and the rest. The blouses or shirts Gemma tended to wear under her suits for official court visits had to stretch to the limit to fasten, the material teasing and testing the hold of the buttons in a clearly provocative manner. As well as that, there was an irresistible freshness about her; thankfully she had ignored the wide-shouldered power-dressing that had become something of a fad for professional women after the success of *Dallas*, the new American soap opera currently obsessing the tabloid press.

In spite of the fact that Mark had been pretty much deprived for almost six years, and arguably might not have been particularly difficult to please, she was certainly equal to anything he could remember, and that included with Justine. He had found it difficult to accept how clearly infatuated he must have been with Justine and over his years away he had become convinced that she had been the real cause of his downfall. It felt good that at last he could see she hadn't been so special and that Gemma was more than a match. Gemma's approach to sex had taken him by surprise – it was a strange but exciting mixture of absolute baseness, along with an almost prudish coyness. On the one hand, he found her appearance radiated an innocence and freshness that suggested a cosseted upbringing. Almost by contrast, and while attempting to impress her with his literary knowledge and general sensitivity, he had discovered that she had read Nabokov's *Lolita* as well as *Justine*, *Juliette* and all of de Sade's English translations that she could get hold of, and that she wasn't interested in the more conventional and popular examples of romantic books and dramas. Somewhat bizarrely, it was after one impromptu and pretty wild session that Mark realised it had been watching a documentary on the life of chimpanzees that had turned her on; and she had admitted that watching animals just doing it was enough for her to lose any inhibitions. Mark wondered if it was because he was getting older or just easier to please himself, but within a few months he felt an attraction and closeness which took him by surprise and which had an air of authenticity that he had never really experienced before.

Getting to know Gemma before and since his release had certainly changed Mark's plans for his future, although if he was being honest he hadn't really had much of a long-term or clearly worked out plan at all. Anyway, *que sera*, as it seemed to be turning out; he realised Gemma was good for him and he'd been lucky, even though he reckoned he deserved it.

In fact, although he had his own flat, it wasn't long after his release before he and Gemma were spending most nights in the same bed, and had decided to buy a place and live together. House prices were still rising at almost ten per cent a year and Mark was keen to invest what money he had as soon as he could. They had decided on Petworth and found a quaint two-up, two-down at the end of a row of four what would originally have been agricultural workers' houses; the sort of Victorian terraced cottages that were found all over the English countryside. The original, outside toilet had been replaced with a kitchen and shower-room extension in the early 1960s and with the exposed beams and open fireplace it maintained a charm and homeliness which both he and Gemma had been taken with. Conveniently, it was on the Littlehampton side of the town, and the move itself had gone through pretty quickly. Neither of them had to sell and they had moved in together within six months of Mark's leaving Ford Open Prison.

***

As his mind returned to the barbecue that Friday afternoon, all in all Mark felt quite positive about life. Even though there had been the odd moments of tension between them – usually about his lack of work and direction, which were becoming a little more regular recently – he was looking forward to Gemma getting back from her work. It was a lovely hazy day which always helped his mood, and now that there was some sign of life from the briquettes, things didn't seem too bad. On the whole, it was comforting to reminisce about the last seven or so months, and his earlier sense of despondency seemed perhaps rather indulgent. It hadn't been long after his release before Mark had also come to feel something close to affection for Littlehampton, in spite of its unmistakably down-at-heel image — maybe, perhaps, because of it. Wandering around the town, he had liked coming across the occasional commemorative plaques highlighting the Roman occupation of the area. He and Gemma had spent a few weekend lunchtimes eating in the slightly forlorn seaside cafés or harbour-side pubs, sometimes along with random groups of ageing bikers who seemed to see Littlehampton as a sort of emblem of bygone, and missed, days. Gemma's rented apartment on Pier Road had been particularly cool and was a class above his own; the elegant main room overlooked the river and lighthouse, and beyond that the Channel. They'd spent some intense but special evenings there at the start of the year and of their relationship, including listening to John Lennon songs in the wake of the shock of his murder; he particularly remembered playing Roxy Music's version of 'Jealous Guy' time after time.

However, after the first couple of months of freedom, as the new year had gathered momentum, and tempering a little his positive mood and feeling as the barbecue at last sprang into life with some gusto, there hadn't been that much to get particularly excited about. Sure, they had bought the house together and the move to Petworth had been something of an adventure, but that had been about it. It wasn't as if he hadn't tried to get his life moving again, but if he was honest about it the latest endeavour, dabbling in the antiques business, showed little signs of taking off for him, and was basically just another example of self-indulgence.

Maybe he had expected it to be too easy, but he assumed with his background as a university lecturer and with two degrees he'd be able to pick up something, and if nothing else some part-time lecturing at least. In fact, after the Christmas break he had given that a go and had made appointments at a couple of local further education colleges to offer his services – the problem was trying to explain a six-year gap in his CV and avoiding having to fill in any awkward questions on application forms about previous convictions. His first attempt, at the College of Technology in Worthing, had been unsuccessful; indeed, he was left with the distinct impression that the two full-time, General Studies lecturers who had met him felt he was over-qualified and potentially some kind of threat to them. After that, he had managed to talk himself into being given a two-hour evening class teaching General and Communication Studies to a group of engineering apprentices at the Chichester College of Technology – a typically uninspired example of 1960s architecture, soulless square blocks with not a curve in sight. The course itself was apparently a compulsory module on some kind of vocational training programme they were enrolled on, but the students themselves had absolutely no interest in improving their communication or general skills. Mark had soon realised why he had been offered those hours. He had struggled through sessions from January till Easter and it had been more than enough to put him off that career path. It had been how he could imagine taking an F stream in some sort of failing comprehensive would be, except that these students were adults, supposedly. Although not overtly aggressive their obvious disdain came over with a slightly threatening air; in particular, he hated having no sensible response to questions about the relevance of it all. One of the most amusing books he'd read while serving his sentence had been *Wilt*; and Tom Sharpe's description of Henry Wilt's experiences of trying to teach literature to bored apprentices in what must have been a very similar type of college had certainly captured the tone of his own brief encounter with similar students. He remembered with some fondness, and maybe slightly rose-coloured glasses, the buzz of teaching bright undergraduates at Sussex University before he'd thrown it all away. He realised how he had revelled in the respect, bordering on admiration, that came with that status; and there had been the added bonus of plenty of young, attractive and impressionable students.

Apart from the academic world which wasn't looking a likely prospect, drugs was about the only other area Mark had any sort of background in, having dabbled with buying and selling when he was a student himself. In fact, soon after getting out of Ford and with little else to do, Mark had looked up a couple of contacts he'd had in Brighton but to little avail. They'd given up dealing and settled down – it was probably no surprise that the hippy dream was certainly becoming a thing of the past. He had to face it, he was well out of touch with that scene. Even though Mark was aware that it smacked of desperation he had also tried unsuccessfully to get some help in that direction from one of his old university mates, Martin, who had always been well-connected. Their reunion meeting had turned out to be a slightly uncomfortable affair, though; Martin's record business was going well and he'd been friendly enough on the surface but there had definitely been an awkwardness between them. In fact, it had left Mark feeling quite down – he and Martin had shared many evenings drinking and getting wasted in the old days, just after Mark had started his job at Sussex University and before Justine and his prison sentence, but on this occasion Martin had seemed distracted and keen to get rid of him. Of course Martin was busy with his work but they hadn't met up for over six years and Mark had hoped for a little more than what felt distinctly like a brush-off. Martin had said enough to suggest that hearing about the murders had both amazed and horrified him; as it apparently had for most of their old friends. He did manage to find out that Martin, Tom, Paul and the rest still met up regularly and that Justine and Tom were still together and apparently on the point of getting married. Martin had clearly felt somewhat embarrassed by the whole thing and had dodged answering Mark's suggestion that he bring Gemma over to meet up and perhaps have a meal or drinks together.

Mark had driven back to Littlehampton afterwards feeling a complete outsider – they might consider themselves open-minded and hip, but serial murdering was obviously a step too far for his old friends. He'd been close to them all for years, but they had all had it easier than him from the start. Most of his university friends had come from public school backgrounds and well-off families and had all managed to do pretty well for themselves in various legitimate pursuits, including property management and the music business. When all had been going along smoothly for himself, Mark had enjoyed their self-confidence and entrepreneurial spirits; and with his position as a university lecturer and published academic he had felt at least their equal. He could see it had never been a real equivalence, though, and maybe they'd always felt it; they possessed and paraded their own hubris with irritating ease. Background and family status clearly still gave a different and unique kind of arrogance. Anyway, to hell with them, he had his life to get on with.

***

Mark looked at his watch. It was half past five, the sun was still hot on his back and playing on the grass in the field behind the house – surely more than ready for a first cut and bailing for hay. He was glad he'd put his shorts on. Gemma couldn't understand his reluctance to show his legs but he'd never been comfy with it, unless he'd been on a beach. He had worn jeans, or between 1975 and 1981 the prison equivalent, ever since he was a teenager and he saw little reason to change the habit. The compromise had been to cut an old pair of Wranglers off just above the knee, and to be fair it felt quite good today.

He reckoned Gemma would be back in ten minutes or so – time to put the burgers and a couple of pork chops on the grill. He still couldn't quite shake off a restlessness that had been with him on and off for a while, and was becoming more on of late, and that was reflected in his mood that afternoon as it veered from contentedness to despondency. It was well into summer and he needed to be doing more than filling time; he'd already done enough of that to last for a lifetime. It had been too easy to let things drift, though. He was becoming too used to basically just pottering around in a desultory but often really quite pleasant way – doing the shopping and cooking, checking local sales and ads. He still had some savings and Gemma's salary covered the mortgage and other bills. And he always managed to find something to keep him at least semi-occupied. There was that year's Ashes series to watch and it had been difficult to take his eyes off the third test which had finished a few days ago. The cricket had been unbelievable: England were following on and heading for defeat when Ian Botham played a remarkable innings, 149 runs from 148 balls; then Bob Willis had taken eight wickets, the Australians were bowled out for 111 and the series was levelled. It had been pretty compulsive viewing as well as taking care of a good part of the day and he couldn't wait for the next match, but it wasn't moving his life on. Then a couple of weeks before that he'd got side-tracked following the street-fighting and rioting in Liverpool and Manchester. While it might not have had much impact on day-to-day life in rural Sussex, Mark had been gripped by the social significance of it, as well as the anger and hatred shown toward Margaret Thatcher and her government. He could imagine the sociologists he had worked with attempting to analyse and explain it all; no doubt it would encourage a glut of conference papers and PhD proposals. He'd had to fight the fleeting nostalgia he still felt for that life – fair enough, a lot of it might have been the emperor's new clothes but it was comfy enough and held a certain cachet.

If he was honest about it and even though he wouldn't call his current lifestyle unpleasant, Mark couldn't ignore the fact that he was beginning to harbour the occasional concern, or maybe more accurately realisation, that living with Gemma was perhaps not really what he had expected when he'd been planning and fantasising about his life after prison. She was gorgeous and sexy, but maybe not as pliable or, although he hated to admit it, as controllable as he would have liked. Typically, though, Mark was too bothered about his own situation and feelings to give any of his slight doubts more than a momentary acknowledgement before storing them away in the recesses of his consciousness. So what if Gemma didn't seem to be as easily impressed with him as he'd imagined she had been? That was life, no doubt. Anyway, the way he remembered it she had pretty much thrown herself at him so he had nothing to reproach himself for there. The niggling worry, though, was that he'd got his character assessments spectacularly wrong before, of course. Gemma had made one or two throwaway comments lately that were playing on his mind: nothing specific, but comments the gist of which seemed to be that given the money her family, or more accurately mother, had, she didn't see why she should be the one working while he managed to occupy himself doing basically nothing. He hadn't really dwelt on them; although he certainly might have if he had taken the time to consider how Gemma's take on things was developing.

***

It had been yet another long, hot and pretty tiring afternoon session at the Chichester Magistrates' Court for Gemma. The court itself was an unimposing square block of a building whose main claim to fame had been the appearance there in 1967 of Mick Jagger and Keith Richards, for committal to Crown Court after their arrest at Richards' country house, Redlands in West Sussex, for various drug offences. They had both turned up at the court to plead not guilty and elect for a trial by jury and been faced with a scrum of fans and media reporters outside the building. Although that had been fourteen years ago it was still talked about with some affection by the clerks and receptionists who'd been around at the time. Indeed, the number of celebrities supposedly involved appeared to grow as memories faded, as did the notion that it was all an establishment-organised attack on the Rolling Stones, fuelled by what sociologists might have termed a 'moral panic' over the group's influence on the youth of the country and over hippies in general. Carole on the front desk had kept her newspaper clippings of the event in her desk drawer and insisted on reminiscing about them at any opportunity, seemingly forgetting that Gemma had seen them on her first visit as well as most subsequent ones too.

That particular day's burglary case against Gemma's client, Christopher Jones, an emaciated ex-drug addict, hadn't attracted the same media frenzy that the Stones had. Even the regular reporter for the *Chichester Observer* hadn't bothered to show up. Apart from the duty solicitors only an equally skeletal-looking girl had turned up; although a few years younger than Christopher she was presumably his partner. Gemma had prepared her report and, she liked to think, delivered it with some style. It was clear to her prison was not the best place for Christopher to end up, and she had made a strong case for a Community Sentence. However, his appointed solicitor that day, Mr Lane, was not one of her favourites and had obviously been more interested in getting away from the court as soon as he could. He had offered little in the way of mitigation even though Christopher had owned up, pleaded guilty and saved everyone a lot of bother as well as expense. When the leading magistrate started to deliver a sentence of imprisonment for one year Gemma resolved to try to avoid working with Lane again, but the added 'suspended for two years' at least provided some satisfaction for her involvement.

She gathered her files together, had a quick word with Christopher, reminding him that any future misdemeanours would automatically revoke the suspension and lead to prison, and went out into the car park and afternoon sun. It was nice enough to put the roof down on her MG midget and boded well for the barbecue Mark said he was going to prepare later. She pulled out of Chichester town centre and on to the old Roman Road and then the A285 to Petworth. There was no need for her to get back to the office in Littlehampton today. She was grateful that her current boss, Gregory, didn't mind her doing her paperwork at home; although she reckoned he must be getting on for sixty, it helped that he obviously fancied Gemma. She didn't mind that, though; at least he wasn't obviously pervy about it. She wondered what it was with men of a certain age, or to be fair any age. The drive itself was a pleasant and picturesque one, right through the best of the South

Downs, but that afternoon in court had convinced her even more strongly that it was time for a change; she didn't intend or need to continue to do what she'd just gone through for that much longer.

In essence, Gemma was pretty much bored with the probation job, and perhaps as a consequence of that, or perhaps anyway, with her life in general. Toward the end of her final year at university, not having much idea of what to do next, she had sort of drifted into it. There had been an advert on one of the university notice boards for a recruitment fair of some kind and Gemma had gone along for no particular reason; she'd picked up various bits of information and leaflets from the different stands, including an application form to work as a probation officer. She had been told by the probation representative that there were good opportunities for graduates and that you could specify what areas you wanted to work in. One of the more interesting courses on her degree had been on crime and society and had involved considering how best to deal with repeat offenders. Perhaps because of that passing interest, Gemma had decided to give it a go and fill the form in, specifying anywhere in the south of England. It had been something of surprise when she was invited to Littlehampton for an interview only a few weeks after graduating with her upper second degree in Sociology. It wasn't that she particularly needed to work, she was well provided for from her father's will but she couldn't face going to live with her mother in the old family home in Farnham. While that might have been comfortable enough, watching her mother's embarrassingly desperate attempts to stay young – and, even more excruciatingly, available – was not on her agenda. Gemma had never got on particularly well with her mother anyway but after the way she had treated her father before he died it had become more than that. Over the last few years Gemma had become convinced that her mother was to blame for her father's death and also for his general and obvious unhappiness. Since going away to university soon after her father's death, her feelings of indifference had developed into something closer to hatred and she had recently felt a strong and growing desire for revenge of some kind.

As it was, the interview itself had gone pretty well. It had really been more of a conversation with the senior probation manager, David, and the administrator-cum-secretary, Lizzie, at the Littlehampton office. Gemma had always got on well with older people, particularly men, and it had been apparent from the start they were pretty desperate for new staff in the West Sussex region. David was clearly quite taken with her – in a nice, avuncular, if slightly drooling, way. He was an earnest, old school-style probation officer who was probably in his early sixties and approaching retirement; it came over that he clearly felt more than a little disillusioned by recent changes to the probation system. Gemma had the sense to play on this and stress the importance of rehabilitation, and of working on a personal rather than managerial level with offenders. She noted his nod of approval when she mentioned the importance of offenders facing up to the consequences of their behaviour and taking responsibility, but that this could only work in a supportive environment. Lizzie was common sense personified; even though she was a

'Miss' and no doubt had always been so, she looked as if she would be the ideal partner, if not wife, for David. It struck Gemma that they probably ran the office like a well organised home, and that gave her a good feeling about the place and job.

Gemma had made the right impression on both of them and sailed through the interview. Although sexism was still rife, the Sex Discrimination Act and the establishment of the Equal Opportunities Commission a few years earlier had made things a little easier; and it had helped that the probation service was one area where women were getting some kind of foot in the door and recognition, compared to many other areas of professional work, at least. So she had walked into the job with little planning, or even thought, really. It had been summer 1980 and Mark had been one of her first assignments. Initially she had gone along to the prison visits to observe and be mentored by David as part of her induction period, but David's disillusionment had been getting to him and he announced he was taking early retirement only a couple of months after Gemma had started to work there. It had seemed sensible for Gemma to carry on with Mark and with preparing his parole report as one of her first proper clients. She had been a little disappointed that David left so soon after her appointment but it had helped that his replacement as her line manager, Gregory, was only a year or two younger than his predecessor and didn't seem keen to change things around too much.

That was over a year ago, and although there was nothing intrinsically wrong with the job, she had had enough. Initially David had been good to work with: he cared for what he did and worked hard too. Apart from him though, the rest of her colleagues had proved something of a mixed bag. Mathew, who'd taken over the official rehabilitation of Mark when they had moved in together earlier in the year, she found particularly irritating. He had cultivated a ponytail to go with a straggly beard that never seemed to be without the remains of his breakfast or lunch, depending on the time of day, and he wore what she assumed from the reek was the same check shirt for days on end. It wasn't so much his appearance or slightly stale odour that grated most with her, but his rather ridiculous and supercilious manner with his colleagues as well as his clients, along with his half-baked advocacy of anti-psychiatry, which he appeared to believe offered some kind of way forward for probation. Even though she knew why he did it, the way that Mark played up to Mathew's unwarranted intellectual snobbishness also really irritated her. On top of that Mathew had tried it on with her when she'd given him the benefit of the doubt and met up with him one evening soon after starting her job.

Her new boss, Gregory, was bearable in small doses; and to be fair his heart was in the right place, he didn't throw his weight around and, more crucially, he seemed to trust her to get on with things on her own. He'd been parachuted in after David's retirement and was a typical example of the ex-army personnel who still made up a good proportion of the service; at least he was at the opposite end of the political and ideological spectrum from Mathew. Gregory had brought in as his deputy Howard, a colleague he had worked with in Portsmouth, also ex-army and, as with so many of them, apparently unable to get a job in the police so settling for this as the next best. Along with Lizzie and Jude, a new and seemingly empty-headed part-time worker whom Mathew was busy homing in on now that he'd accepted that Gemma was out of bounds, that was the team.

Surprisingly it was the clients themselves whom she did feel some degree of sympathy with, and generally speaking they clearly did need support to get on with their lives. There had been a few times when it had felt really good to get a result and to see some progress and it did actually feel like she was making a difference, but it didn't make up for the rest of the job. Aside from her less than inspiring colleagues, the service itself was becoming increasingly bureaucratised and managerialist – the recent emphasis on targets and performance indicators seemed to suit Gregory's style of management and it was a trend that Gemma could see was bound to continue. It was time for her to take control of her life and to do some of the things she had always intended to; and to get what she felt she deserved. And a part of that would involve getting some degree of restitution – it sounded better than revenge – for her father, or perhaps in truth more for her. Although she hadn't thought about it in any great depth, something told her that she needed to start to work on sorting out Mark and getting some kind of benefit from being with him.

As she drove past the old parish church at Duncton, a couple of miles from their cottage, Gemma was amazed how quickly the half-hour drive home had flashed by as she pondered the next step of her life. On one level it was so far so good: the job had been a diversion, a stepping stone maybe, but that was all; and being with Mark had turned out pretty much as she had imagined. He hadn't managed to get anything much going in his post-prison life and had proved reasonably easy to manipulate. That made it sound horribly cold and calculating, which wasn't really the case. They had had some good times together and she did actually care for him; as she mulled over her tentative plans for the future there was a twinge of guilt, but she knew she could manage that.

Soon after they had got together properly, Gemma had taken Mark to meet her mother and as she had expected the two of them had hit it off immediately. Anne was easily flattered and Mark was an inveterate flirt. Thinking back, Gemma hadn't done that with any detailed strategy in mind, although perhaps there had been some kind of nascent intuition that it might be useful, even beneficial in the future.

When she had first visited Mark at Ford Open Prison and started working on his parole application – initially with David taking the lead while she was learning the ropes, and then on her own – she had let him, indeed encouraged him, to find out about her own background and life. It was just a matter of letting the man think he was in control. Come to think about it, that was about the only skill she had ever picked up from her mother, and even if it wasn't one to be particularly proud of, it had its uses. Alongside going through the usual issues and motions involved in sorting out the probation report for Mark, she had initially and at the time purposely painted him a picture of her supposedly idyllic and happy childhood, with devoted and loving parents who gave her everything she wanted. It was, in fact, a picture that was a far cry from the loneliness of a single child, emotionally ignored but materially spoilt by her mother, and an unseen party to the constant whingeing and arguing between her embittered mother and despairing father. Even now she wasn't certain just what was behind her idea to mislead Mark or whether it had even been intentional; however, in attempting to highlight a comfortable and well-off family background, Gemma realised that she had perhaps overdone things and would have to let Mark know something of her real feelings about her mother in due course.

She remembered her father with great fondness; he had been her hero, really. She missed him terribly. He had always had time for her. When she was younger, on returning from his daily commute to work in the city, he would pull back into the driveway of their detached house in Lynch Road, on the south side of Farnham, and always come straight up to her room to check whether she was asleep and to read to her if she wasn't. Even when she had been asleep she had woken the next morning and imagined she'd seen him at the door. He had worked long hours in the city and looking back Gemma realised that he must have been driven to distraction and despair by her mother; no doubt his work had been something of a welcome escape for him. She felt a surge of bitterness; and now she would never have him to turn to if things got tough, or to share the special moments of her life with. Although she had no particular interest in getting married, the thought of doing that without a father just wouldn't seem right.

Anne, Gemma's mother, was a wealthy woman in her own right. She had been left a near fortune from both her father, George, and then her Uncle Arthur, each of whom had held senior positions as well as substantial shares in the Cunard shipping line. Their father, and Anne's grandfather, Cecil, had worked his way up in the famous White Star shipping line in the early years of the twentieth century and had become a director when it had merged with Cunard in the mid-1930s. He had started working at Oceanic House, just across from Trafalgar Square, as a junior clerk soon after Thomas Ismay – the chairman since the founding of the Oceanic Steam Navigation Company, more commonly known as the White Star Line – had died and been replaced by his son Joseph Bruce Ismay in the last year of the nineteenth century. Cecil came to the attention of J Bruce Ismay, as he liked to be known, along with the rest of the senior management, for the way in which he took charge of dealing with the public outcry following the sinking of the Titanic in April 1912. Hundreds of relatives and friends of passengers as well as general onlookers had descended on Oceanic House in the days after the sinking and Cecil had helped to avoid a public relations disaster for the company by ensuring the speedy and sensitive release of appropriate information. Initial reports had been confused and there had been a suggestion that the Titanic was being towed into New York. It wasn't until the day after that there was confirmation of the extent of the disaster. Cecil had spent most of the week virtually living in the White Star offices and offering what news and comfort he could to the waiting crowd.

As well as being the flagship for White Star, it was no doubt due to the Titanic being to a large extent Ismay's project and dream that Cecil's response to the disaster came to his attention. Indeed, the chairman had himself sailed on the ill-fated maiden voyage and been one of the just over seven hundred survivors after being picked up by the RMS Carpathia steamship. It was little surprise that Anne's grandfather's actions in helping deal with the fall-out led to his promotion to a managerial role soon after; and so to his decision to invest all he could in buying shares in the company. After becoming a director in due course, Cecil used his influence to find positions with the company for both his sons just prior to the Second World War and left them his shares when he eventually died in 1938. Although they both survived the war, Anne's father and her uncle, a confirmed bachelor, died within a year of each other in the late 1950s. Anne was the sole heir, her own mother having died in 1949 of cervical cancer, still pretty much undiagnosable let alone untreatable at the time.

An only child brought up in a privileged environment, Anne was self-centred, selfish and arrogant. She had homed in on Jeffrey Powell, her future husband, in the mid-1950s at a party to celebrate the completion and delivery of the Saxonia Carmania, the first of four Cunard liners which had been commissioned by the company to sail on the Atlantic route to Canada. Almost seven years older than her, he worked in the accounts department at Cunard. He was handsome but considerably less well-off than her – an ideal combination, Anne had felt at the time. They had got married in late 1954 and chosen Farnham as the place to buy their first house. Anne had a hankering for suburban living, increasingly in vogue at the time, and Farnham looked to be an ideal location: within reasonably easy reach of the Cunard offices in London but far enough away from the capital to feel it. It was a substantial detached property built a few years previously and lived in by just the first owner and then for a couple of years only. Even though her father was not particularly convinced of Jeffrey's suitability as a future son-in-law, he had provided a substantial deposit for the house as their wedding gift, leaving only a small mortgage to be based on Jeffrey's fairly average salary. He had also made sure that his daughter got the very best and the wedding was a lavish affair. With both her father and uncle highly regarded in the company, the wedding was attended by most of Cunard's senior staff. The ceremony was held at St Andrew's, the imposing Parish Church of Farnham, dating back to the 12th century and according to parish records a milestone on the medieval Pilgrim's Way between Winchester and Canterbury. It had been followed by a reception at the Frensham Pond Hotel, a magnificent building overlooking Frensham Great Pond and with parts of it dating back to the fifteenth century. Previously known as The White Horse its sense of history was enhanced by it having served as a smart and welcome billet for Canadian soldiers serving with the Allies in the Second World War.

Over the years since then, Anne had used every opportunity to throw in Jeffrey's face the fact that it was her family who had the money and who had provided the house and the rest. She had used that strategy to force Jeffrey to attend to her every need and had never wasted the opportunity to demean him and his background, even if in what she convinced herself was a playful manner, and especially whenever they were meeting with or entertaining any friends or family.

Although she hadn't been aware of it at the time, years later as she reviewed her feelings, Gemma had realised that her mother had no real interest in her and didn't really enjoy motherhood, and especially the restraints it might have put on her. However, these could hardly be deemed onerous, particularly as most of the domestic work had been farmed out to nannies, cooks and cleaners. The only times Gemma could remember laughing and playing at home had been when her father was with her. Even that would have been manageable if it hadn't been for the way her mother had treated her dad when he became ill, which had occurred when Gemma was old enough to be aware of what was happening. Although Jeffrey was only in his mid-fifties, heavy smoking had caught up with him, as with many men of his era, and lung cancer had taken hold. Looking back it appeared to Gemma that Anne had seen her husband's illness and subsequent death as an opportunity to move on and essentially had done her best to ignore both her husband and her daughter. She had gone on mini-holidays and nights out with Ruth – Anne's best friend, a would-be socialite who was distantly related to the Cunard family and had become friendly with Nancy Cunard, the only child of the Cunard Line heir Sir Bache, in the years before her death in 1965. Ruth had her own apartment on New Bond Street in the West End and Gemma recalled that Anne seemed to be spending more and more time there once her husband became ill. Sure, Anne had paid for private treatment for Jeffrey but that was doubtless only for appearances' sake and as some sort of salve for her conscience. By the time Gemma reached her mid-teenage years and even before her father's illness had taken hold, she had grown to hate the pretentiousness of her mother, and of Ruth for that matter. On top of her swanning around while Gemma's dad was dying, her mother had decided to take up golf and had joined 'The Sands', better known as the Farnham Golf Club, no doubt seeing it as another opportunity for social networking and climbing.

In part because it was expected from the upper sixth formers of Farnham Girls Grammar School, but also to avoid living in the family house with her mother, soon after her father's death in 1976 Gemma had gone straight to university and then on to her probation job. Although Surrey University was only a few miles away in Guildford, Gemma had made sure she got a place in the halls of residence for her first year and had never moved back to Farnham. However, she had determined at her dad's funeral that she would get some sort of revenge on her mother in due course. She would never forgive the way her dad had been left knowing his wife was more interested in moving on and socialising than caring for him.

It was odd how all of that played back in her mind on the journey back from court that Friday afternoon. She wasn't going to forget her father or let her mother get away with how she'd treated him; and, unbeknown to him, Mark would be given a big part to play in helping her carry it all through. As she turned into the parking space alongside their cottage – one of the benefits of it being an end terrace property – she could smell and hear the barbecue and see the smoke drifting invitingly over the side gate into their back garden. Before getting out of her car she dabbed a bit of her oddly-named Opium perfume around her wrists and ears – Gemma thought it was strange that perfume manufacturers used class A drugs to label their products. Gemma felt good that she had made a decision of sorts about her future.

As she wandered into the garden, Gemma could see that Mark was wearing his compromise for shorts, cut away jeans, and a white T-shirt and was oblivious to anything other than the task in hand. Gemma felt a twinge of guilt: he looked happy and really quite cool. He really had no idea of what had been going on in her head ever since she'd sat with her then boss, David, in one of the interview rooms at Ford Prison and helped prepare Mark's parole application. In actual fact, she had really quite enjoyed helping him sort himself out after his release and then them becoming a couple; and even if it wasn't true love she had certainly felt some affection for him. It might have been manipulative but in spite of his gullibility to any kind of flattery it had been good fun as well; and to be fair he was better company and better in bed than the various males she had hooked up with at university and since. Nonetheless, Gemma had her motivations and felt they were more than merited; and anyway, they didn't necessarily preclude some sort of a future for Mark and her. She was prepared to see how things went.

She crept up on him and put her arms round his chest.

'Hi, you look cool! I hope you've got something ready to drink too.'

'Yes there's some white wine in the fridge, or else a lager if you'd prefer.'

He was quite domesticated too, which had impressed Gemma. He knew that she would have had a trying day at court and had prepared an inviting-looking side salad to go with the burgers and chops sizzling and spitting away on the barbecue.

Gemma poured herself a glass of Riesling and pulled the somewhat rickety wooden table they had found in the shed into position. Although the shadows were beginning to lengthen it was still a lovely, slightly muggy summer evening. Mark served up his culinary effort; even though food always seemed to taste better when eaten outdoors, it was still quite impressive. They sat in a couple of fold-out chairs, looking out over the fields that backed onto the row of cottages and watching, a way further on, a herd of black and white Friesians meandering back to the farm buildings for their evening milking.

'You know I do appreciate this, Mark. Let's go down to the pub for a couple of drinks later on. I'm going to go and have a shower and change. Why don't you come and give my back a massage after that, before we go out?'

Mark recognised the invitation as a thinly disguised euphemism and couldn't help smiling; not a bad way to start the weekend, he thought. It was encouraging that it was her idea as well. As usual Gemma certainly looked good in what she termed her 'court clothes' and he couldn't miss the naughty smirk as she brushed past him on her way indoors.

After the initial excitement of the move to Petworth and since living together things had become less spontaneous and even less regular. Of course, he realised that Gemma had a full-time job but then he did more than his share of looking after things. It wasn't that they weren't having sex, just that it less frequently involved her taking the lead. He heard the shower spring to life and felt the usual stirrings as he took their plates to the kitchen sink and topped up their drinks.

It was nice to wash the week away and as she let the water sprinkle through her hair, Gemma knew she'd enjoy Mark sorting her out; and she would enjoy playing her part too. And even if it might be that she was using him, as people would no doubt put it, he was having a bloody good time of it as well. She enjoyed sex and it was a source of pride-cum-duty that she always liked to make sure that her partner did too.

***

Her meeting Mark at Ford Open Prison as he was being considered for parole had presented the glimmer of an opportunity that, perhaps even unknown to herself at first, Gemma had been waiting for ever since her father died. It was apparent that he had made a pretty decent job of poisoning both of his in-laws some years previously; and on reading up on his case she discovered that if he'd have been a bit more together and a better judge of character he would probably never have been found out. Gemma knew she was good-looking and had played on that of course, and played on him. Without having any definite plan but just an inkling that he could perhaps help her somehow, she had homed in on Mark as a potential ally in getting back at her mother, even perhaps getting rid of her. Rather pathetically, too, she actually quite liked playing along to the part of a soft, naïve and impressionable young woman coming to terms with work in the 'real' world. At the same time she had to admit that she had liked the looks he gave her on her first visit to Ford. Of course, there wasn't much competition given he had been in prison for around six years, but he had an air of self-confidence bordering on arrogance that she liked, as well as a bit of class too, and he was obviously reasonably intelligent – and, to be fair, reasonable-looking as well. She had expected to be dealing with offenders who had problems reading and writing rather than those with post-graduate qualifications and university teaching experience.

As well as that, though, Mark had proved remarkably easy for her to manipulate. She smiled to herself as she remembered the way he had lapped up her massaging of his ego when he was telling her about the supposedly famous sociologists he'd known and worked with. They might have written the odd, fairly readable and indeed arguably erudite text – and she had enjoyed parts of her Sociology degree at Surrey too – but they were hardly iconic figures of the age or even household names. Harold Garfinkel, David Matza and the like were unlikely to be recognised and mobbed on the streets; and their work might not have moved humankind on a great deal. Nonetheless Sociology had given Gemma and Mark some common ground and getting to know him had proved more fun than she had imagined it would – he had more about him than her previous dates and boyfriends. Actually, it made her quite horny thinking of how she'd managed things since meeting him and since his release last November. She realised that she had been rubbing the soap between her legs for longer than usual and shouted to Mark to come up and see to her. No harm in mixing pleasure with scheming. As she waited for him she found herself pondering briefly on the difference between revenge and vengeance. Maybe revenge implied something more personal and more equivalent too, a sort of balancing out of things. Vengeance could be disproportionate, gratuitous even. It could go over the top.

Anyway, Gemma was quite prepared to take her time: if she had to play the long game, fair enough, but she wasn't going to forget and she was determined and certain that she'd get what she wanted in the end. Even though Gemma had purposely not gone into that much detail about her childhood and family life, she had told Mark enough to get him interested. After all, his criminal career had involved manipulating his first set of in-laws and even if she wasn't planning to marry him, her mother was a sort of quasi in-law. Since they had got together after his release, Gemma had hinted pretty strongly that she and her mother were left very well off after her father died, and that her initial description of her childhood as being a happy one was only true in part and that in reality she and Anne had a frosty if not dysfunctional relationship. She passed it off with a little psychological babble about her not being able to face up to and admit to the actuality of her childhood, and how she probably found it more comforting to believe that it had been the way she wanted it to be.

It hadn't taken long for Gemma to start seeing Mark as a partner in more ways than one. Soon after their first few weeks together, she realised that it might well be sensible for Mark and Anne to get along; something told her that at some stage she would need Anne to trust him and perhaps, even probably, fancy him a little. Gemma was well aware of her mother's love of any sort of interest or flattery and of Mark's ability to deliver in that direction.

While there was certainly no love lost between Gemma and Anne, she had to admit that her mother wasn't a bad looking woman. As with so many women of her background and generation, the cigarettes and drink had taken their toll but with a decent amount of make-up and her expensive dresses she did manage to exude a sort of glamour. As well as that, Mark was in his mid-thirties and probably less than twenty years younger than her mum; so really there was only slightly a bigger age gap than between Mark and herself. Strange how it was definitely more acceptable for older men to have younger female partners or lovers; the other way around always seemed to smack of desperation on the one hand or greed on the other – mind you, no doubt there were always exceptions.

Mark's self-belief, which had been apparent even given his situation as a lifer trying for parole, had amused her too. He hadn't thought it odd or even unlikely when she had offered to arrange finding a flat for him in her name, so as to avoid any awkward questions about his past. It seemed he was too full of himself to assume it was anything other than the fact she was absolutely crazy about him and couldn't wait to spend time with him when he got out. She'd been careful not to overdo it, but had started to plant the idea that, as employment prospects for him might not be too great after a lengthy prison term, maybe they could do something together. She hadn't actually, or even yet over half a year on, referred to his pretty sound knowledge of poisoning and murder, but had let slip that maybe they could make use of her family's wealth in some way.

Even before any type of plan had begun to be formulated, Gemma recognised that it would be important to ensure that Mark believed it was he who was the one persuading her – to feed him the ideas and let them take hold and him take over. For now, she must make sure that she and Mark spent more time with her mother, with more regular visits to Farnham. She would have to start to get Anne to trust Mark, but she needed him to know more about how much she hated her mother. Although she had started to hint at it, that was something she hadn't really gone into any detail about with him. The key was that it would have to be Mark who believed he was persuading her to engineer and carry through any sort of plan.

***

Mark appeared at the bathroom door with a couple of glasses of wine.

'I've done some strawberries and cream for after if you want.'

'That's nice. Come on, give me a cuddle; you smell of barbecue and beer. Look, I've been thinking, let's go up to my mum's tomorrow, I need to talk to her about what she's going to do with the house and everything. Thing is, I'm getting a little worried 'cos the last couple of times I've talked to her she's sounded a bit odd, and I'm getting a bit bothered about her desperation to find a new man. Even though she looks a bit of a wreck without her make-up, she's still only in her mid-fifties and I'm not too keen on anyone else homing in on her, and particularly her money.'

That was enough of a hint for now. She wrapped herself in a towel, directed him to the bedroom and lay back and let Mark take over. He really was getting quite adept and seemed to enjoy it too. After she had finished, she undid the buttons on his jeans-cum-shorts, checked he was hard enough and pulled him on top of her. He didn't take long himself.

'I reckon all those years away has certainly improved your technique. I bet you're better than ever now that you've had all that time to appreciate what you were missing.'

There was no harm in a little flattery after all; and he was pretty good, she had to admit.

'Come on, after I've tried your skills in the dessert area let's get dressed and walk into town. I fancy a drink or two tonight.'

***

Although they'd got through another couple of bottles at the Angel Inn in the centre of Petworth and meandered back the half mile or so home well after closing time, Gemma woke up early the next morning. The sun was streaming through the little upstairs cottage window and she could see the cows were already well into their day's munching and chewing. She phoned her mother and said she and Mark fancied a Saturday drive and would call in and bring something for lunch and maybe spend the afternoon there. Even though Anne had an array of helpers, from cleaner to cook to gardener, Gemma said they'd help sort through and tidy up some of the junk that had been left in the garage since Jeffrey died.

Gemma brought a cup of tea up to Mark and reminded him that they had things to do.

'You go down to the garage shop and get some cheese and ham for later, and maybe some of their nice bread. I'll tidy up the barbecue stuff and then we'll head off to Farnham.'

By the time they were ready to go, it was nice enough to have the roof down, so Gemma drove them up in the MG. The twenty or so mile trip would give her the opportunity to continue to work on Mark. The Downs looked spectacular as they drove up to Haslemere and the borders with Surrey and Hampshire before crossing the A3 Portsmouth to London road at Hindhead, which, according to a newly erected welcome sign, was the highest village in Surrey. As they slowed down to negotiate the congestion in the town centre before heading up to Beacon Hill and the Farnham road, she started.

'Look Mark, there's some things about my family you probably need to know. My dad did leave me a decent amount, enough to cover renting the flat in Littlehampton for as long as I wanted and for the car too, but he wasn't particularly wealthy in his own right; the real family money was and still is my mother's. She had all the money as well as a pile of shares from her father and grandfather and from what I've been able to pick up it's a small fortune, close on half a million at least. The house itself may have been hers and Dad's but that's all hers now of course. Anyway, it was mainly her family's money which enabled them to get the house in the first place.'

Mark put down the crossword he'd been toying with.

'Well, sure, I guessed as much. So where does that leave you and us?'

Now she had his attention she pushed on.

'The thing is, Mum and I never got on particularly well and never will. I'm sure you must have picked up on that anyway. And she's so desperate to be the centre of attention I don't trust her with that money. It might seem callous and mercenary but, I mean, it'd be difficult for me if she got herself another man, and from the way she lashes out on her clothes and hair and the rest I think she's got her sights set somewhere. You know if she did re-marry, any inheritance that might come my way could well disappear.'

She'd finished by the time they pulled down through Frensham and were heading toward Farnham. It would be better to leave it to Mark to come up with the idea of the two of them working together to avoid the scenario she'd just presented. Sow the idea and let it grow. Mark might be a bit slow at times but she knew he wasn't stupid.

***

The air of affluence and class was apparent as they negotiated the south side of Farnham before turning into Lynch Lane and the impressive detached houses, almost hidden behind hedged and manicured front gardens.

'Yes, it is bloody impressive down here,' Mark muttered almost to himself.

Gemma could see that Mark's brain was whirring. The *Times* crossword page had long since settled on the floor by his feet.

The family house itself was at the top end of the road, built to a contemporary, but still slightly neo-Tudor style in the early 1950s. It was set in large grounds of at least half an acre; but it wasn't just the house, it was the furniture and contents that also evidenced more than new money. Anne's grandfather had invested in what was at the time modern art: particularly impressive were a couple of Maxfield Parrish paintings he'd brought at some sort of private sale when he was in New York on shipping business in the 1930s. The pictures, 'Winter Sunrise' and 'Hilltop', were hung alongside one another at the top of the staircase. Gemma had pointed them out at his previous and first visit to the house and Mark had resolved to check out the potential value as soon as he got back to Petworth. He had looked into it and had found out that Parrish had died sometime in the 1960s, which made it highly likely that his work must have soared in value since. However, Mark hadn't yet got round to taking his interest any further.

As the house itself came into view, Gemma felt her usual wave of bitterness. She had been brought up there and stayed until she was almost twenty. It should have been the ideal place to grow up but she had few happy memories of it. She'd felt the solitude, almost abandonment, of an only child and had spent hours and days in her room, or else, and particularly when she was younger, in the trees at the bottom of the garden, often escaping there while her mother and father were arguing with one another, or more typically just not communicating at all.

Gemma parked on the gravelled forecourt in front of the garage doors and they let themselves in through the side door and into the kitchen. They found Anne in the sitting room, looking out over the large rear garden, smoking as usual with a couple of her magazines on the occasional table next to her. Gemma noticed *Country Life* and *Vogue*, magazines that had arrived regularly for as long as she could remember. On first impression her mother looked quite elegant and even attractive, but a closer look highlighted the heavily applied make-up doing its best to hide a somewhat ravaged complexion.

As was the norm when Anne was growing up, she hadn't taken much notice of the sun and the fact that her family had been able to enjoy lengthy summer holidays in France and Spain had gradually but inexorably left their mark.

Mark had only met Gemma's mother on a few brief occasions and it struck him that he'd never really looked at the person who possibly – presumably, really – was his potential mother-in-law. On closer inspection, she looked a good deal older than her fifty-five years – or fifty-six, he couldn't remember which. In spite of that, she still retained a certain attractiveness, albeit in a strange sort of way. However, the overall effect was oddly disconcerting; he couldn't quite decide whether it most resembled a kind of faded femme fatale look or, perhaps more accurately, a watered-down type of gothic horror. He could see what Gemma had meant about her not necessarily planning to stay single for ever, or even long. It definitely smacked of a desperate attempt to turn back the years and remain desirable.

Gemma went over and gave her mother a perfunctory kiss on the cheek.

'I'll make some sandwiches and tea for lunch – ham and mustard, if that's okay – then we'll have a go at sorting through a few of Dad's things. You stay there, Mother.'

Anne seemed happy enough to let her daughter take charge.

'That's nice of you, Gemma. Elaine was here to do some cleaning this morning but she never stays longer than a couple of hours on Saturdays and spends most of that time making herself coffee. I sometimes wonder what I'm paying her for.'

Mark trailed after Gemma into the kitchen and put the kettle on.

'Who the hell's Elaine?'

'She's mother's sort of servant really – does a little cleaning and cooking; and washing, ironing and the rest, come to think of it. She was even around when I was a child. It's strange, you know, but thinking about it my mother didn't really seem to do very much at all. As well as that there's even another woman, Alma, who seems to clean once or twice a week as well. Heaven knows what the division of labour is, though.'

Mark thought he'd have a closer look around the house while Gemma was getting lunch organised. He had noticed a few interesting bits and pieces on his only previous visit but hadn't had time or a particular reason to examine them closely. With what Gemma had told him earlier it seemed sensible to check things out properly.

Although there was no discernible pattern or coherence to the furnishings and décor of the inside, it was obvious that there were some pretty pricey items there. The large, open-plan hall had a couple of matching Victorian spoon back chairs, one gentleman's and one lady's, which Mark reckoned must be worth a good £500 each. They still had their original castors as well. He'd have to get the *Miller's Guides* out and check them later. In one of the four rooms off the hall there was what he reckoned to be a mahogany dining table along with six matching carved chairs that were equally impressive and presumably valuable. The study, which

56

clearly hadn't been touched since Jeffrey died a few years back, contained an elegant leather-topped desk and a separate Davenport, as well as a couple of what looked like original Victorian watercolours. In contrast, the chairs and sofas in the sitting room and morning room had presumably been top of the range in the late 1950s but looked out of place and out of time too; and probably of little real value. The 1960s style sideboard and record player were even more incongruous next to a stylish, glass-fronted, and what he reckoned must be late nineteenth-century, walnut bookcase.

As well as the Parrish paintings on the upstairs landing, which he double-checked and resolved to get valued as soon as he could, there was an enormous unattributed landscape done in heavy, dark oils, and an ornate gilt framed mirror. He had no idea about the various china vases and jugs scattered somewhat randomly around the four bedrooms on the first floor – but they'd be worth checking out later.

By the time Gemma called out that lunch was ready, he was well aware that there had been and still was serious money in her family. She caught him at the bottom of the stairs as she was taking a tray of sandwiches through.

'Look Mark, you're good with older women, remember you told me all about you and Jean and how you had her eating out of your hand. Why don't you try your charm on Anne, she'd love a bit of attention and sweet-talking and it might be useful, who knows?'

It crossed Mark's mind that maybe he and Gemma were coming to the same conclusion, or at least thinking along the same lines. He was fed up with not bringing

57

any money in and she had made it clear that being a probation officer was not the be all and end all for her. Obviously he'd have to be the one to take the lead but maybe she wouldn't need much persuading if it came to it. It was all very well thinking he had moved on but things hadn't really happened for him since his release and if he was honest he was getting bored with the lack of direction in his life.

Gemma knew Mark well enough to be pretty sure he'd been weighing up the value of the family's bits and pieces. Once he'd got the idea in his head that it should all come to her, she could just sit back and let him take the lead, with a nudge here and there maybe. The next step would be to let him know she would be pretty jarred off if any of her legacy went elsewhere and to convince him she wouldn't actually give a damn if anything happened to Anne. She perhaps hadn't let her real feelings about her mother come through fully yet. Fair enough, she had laid the groundwork but hadn't really let rip. It wouldn't be difficult to do that: even though her father had died four years ago, the memories of that Easter and early summer of 1977 were as vivid as ever.

She had been nineteen and at the end of a year off after completing her A-levels at Farnham Girls Grammar School; and until then she wasn't sure if she would bother with university. After all, she wouldn't need a career or even a job particularly. That all changed after her dad had gone. She knew that was the end of her family life and another three years as a student would be the obvious and easiest route away.

It had been a short illness and swift decline. He had been diagnosed with lung carcinoma in the March and had died within two months, from what his death certificate termed a pulmonary embolism. It wasn't the unfairness of it that got to Gemma, but the way her mother dealt with it, basically implying that he had been a constant burden and disappointment to her. Gemma had sat with him every day, firstly at Frimley Park hospital and then at home when they'd been told it was too late to do anything other than wait. Meanwhile her mother had taken every opportunity to get away, claiming she couldn't stand illnesses or hospitals and wasn't any good at nursing. She had spent a good few nights out in London, apparently staying over at her friend Ruth's apartment. Particularly galling for Gemma, she had even spent that Easter, when her dad was dying, visiting Joseph, an old friend of her Uncle Arthur's, in his fancy villa, a few miles inland from Benalmadena on the Spanish Costa del Sol. Anne had been her uncle's favourite, indeed only, niece. As Anne had grown older the regular family speculation over his sexuality hadn't bothered her; although that had died down after her uncle's death within a few months of her father's. Maybe Joseph had been a partner to Anne's uncle in more ways than one; and if so, good luck to them, thought Gemma. However, even though Gemma was sure that there wasn't some sort of hideous physical attraction between Joseph and her mother, it was no excuse for her to abandon Jeffrey virtually on his deathbed. It had crossed Gemma's mind that her mother might even have helped her dad's deterioration along – and not just with her attitude. She'd been pretty keen to get him on the prescribed medication and to keep him heavily dosed up on it too.

Gemma couldn't wait until it was her mother's turn; and as far as she was concerned, the sooner the better. Anyway, it was time to galvanise Mark into doing something useful. She knew he'd been having difficulty getting anything going after prison and would be ready to throw himself into helping her sort things out. The thing was, his neediness was beginning to get to her. He obviously saw a long-term future for the two of them and Gemma knew that she'd need to keep that belief going for as long as it took. It would have to be handled delicately – she would have to balance involving him in her plans while starting to prepare him for the fact that as far as she was concerned there was no way they would be together permanently. As ever, though, one step at a time.

She took her mother's plate and cup.

'How about some of that chocolate cake Elaine must have made?'

'No dear, I've had enough, that was very nice.'

'Look Mother, I'm going to go through some of Dad's stuff in the study and then the boxes in the garage. It's been four years now and time to tidy up a bit. Why don't you show Mark around the garden, and then get him to pour you a G & T or something? Maybe even watch a bit of TV and relax. You two should get to know each other a bit.'

There was no harm in encouraging her to drink and smoke. She winked at Mark and left them to it.

***

Mark and Gemma's mother walked down the side of the recently cut lawn alongside the immaculately kept borders. Ever since Anne and Jeffrey had moved in soon after their marriage a little over twenty-five years ago, Jim, their gardener, had done two afternoons a week, whatever the weather. With the hot late summer sun high in the sky, it looked like a show garden, a mixture of lavender, peonies and petunias at the front of the flower beds, then an array of hydrangeas and foxgloves, with larger bushes, rhododendrons and magnolias, at the back.

'My goodness, Anne, this is a lovely spot, you know.'

'Yes, I suppose so. You know, it's odd, I've never really spoken to Jim, the gardener. He just comes, does whatever it is he does, has a cup of tea from his flask and goes. Jeffrey used to spend hours talking to him. I don't even know if he's had a pay rise or anything since Jeffrey's gone, I just leave paying him to Elaine. You're right, though, he has done a pretty good job here. I don't really appreciate it as much as I should.'

Mark couldn't help himself.

'Well, it does look in great shape; the colours are fabulous and they bring out the dress you're wearing, you sort of match them.'

Anne turned towards him and smiled. He really was a nice young man, she was enjoying being in his company and being the centre of attention.

'That's nice of you Mark. As I said, it's awful really but I hardly ever spend any time out here, I just look out and expect everything to be in order.'

Along with the perception that he was acting on auto-pilot, Mark felt a weird sense of *déjà vu*. Anne might have been Jean, his first, assuming for a moment she would be his second, mother-in-law. He'd tried the same sort of lines on Jean almost seven years ago, and also in her garden, near Rottingdean on the Sussex coast and overlooking the Channel, before plying her with drinks and a variety of drugs. If only he hadn't been so fooled by Justine he'd have certainly got away with it and wouldn't have wasted those six years. For the first time what he assumed must have been gradually developing in the back of his mind struck him forcibly; maybe he and Gemma could do things properly, and do them together this time.

Beyond the lawn and the border at the bottom edge of it was the vegetable garden that had been Jeffrey's domain; although Jim had kept an eye on it, it wasn't the gardener's interest or forte really and now it looked tired and quite out of kilter with the rest of the grounds. They wandered past some straggly stems which had presumably hosted sprouts in the past; there were little white plastic sticks indicating what had once been where but the writing on them had long since faded away, much as Jeffrey himself had. Further down, at the end of garden, was almost a mini orchard: four apple trees and the same number of pear trees, with the fruit already visible, and the pears looking as if they'd be ready to pick in no more than a few weeks at the most. Then along the back edge of the grounds a row of silver birch trees and the other side of their boundary fence the back gardens of the equally prosperous houses on Old Compton Lane. It really was very pleasant, somehow relaxing, and Mark felt the first signs of him slipping into a once-familiar, and what he had presumed would be a once-only, role.

'This is gorgeous, Anne. You know, you should have a party here one evening. With your style I know you'd be a great hostess, and after all it's been a long time since Jeffrey passed away. Why not live a little?'

He could see Anne was enjoying herself; but perhaps too soon to suggest something a little stronger than G & Ts and cigarettes, maybe that might come along in due course. She did look in her element.

'Well I suppose you're right, Mark. It has been a good few years since Jeffrey died and I think I'm over it now, you know.'

Mark smiled. Maybe the fact that she was a two-faced so-and-so would help him move things along.

'Come to think of it, we could even go up to town and catch some live music. Gemma told me you liked a bit of jazz when you were younger and they still have some good nights at the Marquee. It's a great place, just off Oxford Street, I used to go there regularly in the early '70s; and it's not just kids there, they cater for a nicely diverse audience. You'd fit in fine.'

Gemma's comment about the potential difficulties, financially anyway, if Anne re-married had been playing on his mind since his pretty perfunctory valuation of the house and its contents. He needed to do a little digging and see what her future plans were and whether she had anyone in mind.

'You could always take someone along and we could go as a foursome. I'm sure you've got a good few admirers.'

Anne lit a cigarette as they finished their tour of the garden and returned to the patio and up to the French windows that opened out onto the back of the house.

'Well I must say I've been out a couple of times with Jenny, an old friend from before I met Jeffrey actually, just for a bite to eat at a nice little restaurant that's just opened up in Guildford and I did get a bit of attention. You know I didn't tell Jenny in case it gave the impression of showing off, but I was even given a phone number by a chap who was chatting to us on one occasion and I have actually met up with him for lunch a couple of times since. He's single, either widowed or divorced – I didn't want to ask – but seems to be a bit of a minor celebrity in Guildford. They all knew him at both restaurants and he's certainly got a nice motor, not sure what but certainly expensive looking. But you know, Mark, and this seems a little big-headed, I felt he was too old for me. I didn't ask him his age of course, but I reckon I could do better and after all in my position I'm not after someone just because of their money.'

Mark played along, and the flannel came out with long-practised and not forgotten ease.

'I'm not surprised Anne, you look bloody good for your age, you know.'

'You're too kind Mark, even if it is just flattery. You know, Gemma's lucky to have you. The thing is, Mark, even though I'm a lot older than you two I still have my needs.'

That was more than enough information for the moment, he needed to think things through. It felt odd: inevitable but also disturbing. It was as if he was watching himself from outside; and this was what he was actually good at – setting the bait, preparing to pounce.

'Well, it's been really nice spending a little time with you today. Let's go back inside and see if Gemma's done. And you know, Anne, as well as going to town for a night out, you could always come down and stay with us in Petworth, you must get a little lonely here by yourself. We'd be pleased to see more of you.'

Gemma had finished sorting through the garage and her dad's study and was leaving the second of two large bags by the outside bin. As Mark and Anne appeared from the back garden, she could see Mark had already taken his new task seriously. He really was pretty adept at manipulating older women; her mum had the self-satisfied demeanour of someone who had been seriously flattered. Gemma almost felt sorry for her.

'Hi you two, I've chucked out all the accounting books and ledgers, they'd be no use to anyone anyway. Why not let Mark try and sell the desk and Davenport, at least? It'll make a bit of space and you don't use them anyway.'

Anne seemed happy with that and Gemma suggested Mark take a picture of them to show to his antique contacts as they were too big to fit in the MG for the trip back. It was time for her and Mark to get serious: she needed to see how much prompting he would need. She guessed very little, as long as he assumed *he* was in control. Today had started things moving but it was probably best not to overdo it too soon.

'Anyhow, we'd best get going, it's been nice to help out and I'll make sure we see more of each other from now on.'

They said their goodbyes and Mark promised to arrange a night out with Anne and also to help her plan and organise an evening do at the house before the end of summer.

***

It was close on five when they left and Gemma suggested she and Mark stop off at a pub on the way back and see if they could get something to eat.

'We could try the Devil's Punchbowl in Hindhead, that's usually pretty good and I'll pay. And I've got to hand it to you, Mark, you really are a smooth operator: from what I could see you were getting on well with my mother and I reckon you've got something up your sleeve already.'

Gemma doubted that Mark had any clear strategy as yet but there was no harm in egging him along and keeping him sweet too. She parked on the London Road, finding a spot right outside the front of the Punchbowl and they ordered from the bar meal menu – it was odd how basket meals had become all the rage over the last year or so. The pub had that early evening air of anticipation, as if it was gearing itself up for a busy Saturday evening. They took their drinks to the window seat and waited for the scampi and chips that both of them had gone for. Gemma wanted to see what Mark had been up to.

'Well look, now you've spent some time with her, do you think I'm right to be a little bit concerned about my mother's intentions, then?'

'Yes I can see your point, she's not going to sit around by herself for ever. At the moment I assume you're in line for it all but you're probably right, that could certainly change. She mentioned this old guy she'd already had a couple of lunch dates with in Guildford. He didn't sound like a gold-digger but you can never tell. Rather bizarrely she said he was too old; and if she was planning on snaring someone younger then I could see that could be a different story.'

It was clear to Gemma that she was right about her mother; it was definitely time to get the plan in the open and to make sure Mark was on the same wavelength. She decided to go for it.

'This might seem callous, and I've never told you this really, but the thing is I've come to actually hate my mother. It was not so much from when I was young, 'cos she didn't really get that much involved with me, with all the helpers she had. It was what she did to Dad. Thinking back, I can remember her constantly moaning at him for this or that. I guess I didn't take much notice of it at the time, but she would go on about him not being rich or successful in his own right, and she'd compare him to her father, of course. It was no wonder he sat and worked or read in his study most evenings. I suppose he had no interest in the type of social networking my mother wanted to get involved with. I remember once when he started playing golf with one of his colleagues who lived out of London like him and she went on and on about him never being around. I think he just gave it up after a few weeks. It came back to me when I saw his clubs and golf buggy lying around in the garage earlier.'

Their food arrived; the claim to be home-cooked might have lacked a little credibility but it looked pretty good all the same, even if the chips would no doubt congeal into the tissues at the bottom of the basket. After they'd decided which of the array of packets of sauces they'd go for, Gemma continued.

'You know, I don't think there is anything wrong with two people just growing apart, and if that had been the case I would have accepted things, but it was how she treated him and what she did when he got ill. I'm ashamed I didn't do anything about it now. I couldn't stand things but just left them to it. She made him feel a burden, I heard her telling him one afternoon when he was back from the hospital how she had wasted her life on him. I don't think she actually told him to hurry up and die but she certainly gave him, and me for that matter, that impression. She was busy contacting private nursing homes as soon as he was back home, as if she was doing him a favour; and if he hadn't gone so quickly she wouldn't have had him hanging around the house, that's for sure.'

Gemma found that saying it out loud was, surprisingly, more painful than she had expected, but she could see Mark was taking it in.

'Look, I won't go on but she made my dad's life unhappy and his death even more so. He told me a few days before he went that I was the only good thing that had happened to him. You know, I really hate her for that; and somehow I want to get her back as well. As

68

well as that I don't really trust her either. I'm not saying she'd leave me with nothing but she'll always put herself and her enjoyment first.'

They sat back and Gemma ordered another beer for him and a glass of wine for herself. Mark looked a little shell-shocked.

'Wow, I knew you weren't close, but I never realised all of that. What a cow; but you mustn't blame yourself, you were too young to do anything.'

Mark wondered if Gemma had guessed what had already crossed his mind. It was worth a try.

'This might seem absolutely crazy but I've been thinking, I wasted over six years in prison and I've not really got anything together since I got out. If you really want to pay her back and get what you deserve too, maybe we could sort something out.'

It was strange but over the years Mark had always referred to murder or death elliptically, he'd never felt able to say it out loud. Come to think of it, 'sorting out' was his favourite euphemism.

'Of course, it is way off the wall and only a thought, and, with my record, hardly feasible.'

Things were working out just as Gemma had planned. That was enough for now. She interrupted him, she needed to reassure him and leave the finer details for the future.

'Mark, you really *would* help me, wouldn't you? That means so much to me; and now we're together we'd both benefit too. I don't know, though, let's not rush into anything. We'll see how things work out.'

She knew how his mind worked and no doubt he'd have thought things through already, but no harm in spelling it out while they were on the subject.

'I know you never thought you'd go back there, Mark, but maybe you're right, and maybe in future we need to make sure we get what we deserve. Let's face it, if it hadn't been for you assuming Justine would support you, things would have worked out fine for you. You were bloody clever. I knew that as soon as I met you at Ford Prison. I actually reckon you could do that sort of thing again without anything pointing to you.'

The irony of it was left in the air for now. They were both well aware of it. It had been little over a year since she had been assigned the task of helping to assess Mark's fitness to be released on licence from a life sentence for the murder of his then in-laws, and after that to help him with his rehabilitation. She pushed on, keeping it at the level of a general idea for the time being.

'You could take charge, you've got the ideas – but you do realise, Mark, if we did do anything I'd support you, I'd be with you absolutely. Anyway, I'm fed up with the probation work, you know that. I want what should be mine anyway; you know my uncle and grandad would have wanted me to have it, they wouldn't expect me to have to work basically as a glorified dogsbody.'

By the time they'd finished their drinks, they were both well aware they'd made some kind of pact. Gemma felt pretty turned on by how it had all panned out. She'd leave it for the time being though.

'Come on Mark, let's get home, I don't know why but thinking about all this has made me bloody horny.'

It was only about fourteen miles from Hindhead back to Petworth and Gemma put her foot down. She looked over at Mark. *He deserves it and so do I. It can be a little bit of advance payment for him, and he's good at it too.* Taking the left fork at Fernland, she pulled hard over into one of the off road tracks heading up toward Castle Copse. She jerked the MG to a halt at the first available gateway.

'Come on Mark, I can't wait.'

She almost dragged him round to the back of the car to a patch of grass by the side of a four bar gate enclosing a field heavily populated with a herd of rich, red-brown Sussex cattle. Mark didn't need much persuading anyway. By the time she'd unbuttoned his jeans and reached into his boxers he was more than hard enough. It was convenient she had chosen a short enough skirt that morning. The grass, weeds and even odd thistle felt good as he pulled her knickers off and rocked in and out of her.

She kissed him.

'Anyway, those cows don't look as if they care too much.'

PART TWO:
AUTUMN 1981 – JANUARY 1982

Friday 11 September 1981

It wasn't as straightforward as him 'reverting to type', to use that somewhat hackneyed psychological concept. If he wanted to rationalise it, then perhaps just 'making up for lost time' was nearer the mark, along with facing up to the frustrations consequent on his having a criminal record and life-sentence for murder. Generally speaking, Mark appreciated structure and clear planning over spontaneity and impulsivity; however, he was well aware that it wasn't always easy to categorise everything that neatly, and sometimes structures needed circumventing. The circumstances had been different when he had to do everything himself and keep Justine out of it. For one thing, Gemma was more reliable: she wasn't just a fling or even a paramour, they were a proper couple, they'd been living together for the best part of a year. More to the point, they were doing this together, she was right behind him – almost encouraging him, when he thought about it. In fact, it was unlikely he would be where he was today if Gemma hadn't sowed the seeds.

Mark was sitting in the oak panelled reading room of Chichester Library. He'd decided to spend the day doing some research and planning. They had driven down from Petworth that morning and he had dropped Gemma off at her office in Littlehampton just under fifteen miles away, arranging to pick her up later. Even though she had been getting increasingly fed up with her job, Gemma had decided to carry on for a few more months at least, to see how things panned out with Mark and her mother before making any final decisions. Mark's intention was to read up on suspicious deaths and in particular poisonings that had taken place over the years since he'd been given his prison sentence. Even though they hadn't really thought things through in any great detail, he felt the need to push on with what he now felt of as *their* plan. Amongst other things he wanted to check out what advances there might have been in forensics and detection. However, for the last hour or so he had been side-tracked by the daily papers.

Ever since he was growing up in Brighton, libraries had held a difficult to explain fascination for Mark, and particularly the reading rooms with the daily national and local papers spread out on massive desks and an array of sensible sounding magazines and journals covering all kinds of interests and hobbies arranged on display stands around the room. He remembered having done a lot of his school work in Brighton Library, walking up from the Seven Dials after school and then meandering down North Road, past the newsagents, second hand shops and record stores that gave that part of Brighton a special feel in the early 1960s. He'd felt comfortable sitting amongst the motley collection of people who had frequented the reading room there. At the time, Mark hadn't realised that a good few of the regulars who seemed to sit there for most of the day were using it as their second, and sometimes only, home. However, they were only a part of the clientele; there were also what he had liked to think of as intellectuals doing important research and then there were other teenagers, some from his grammar school but also girls from Varndean. One year, it must have been around nineteen sixty-two or three, there'd been a girl called Grace, he'd only found out her name after months of sitting around the same table, usually between half four and half five and before going home for tea. She had long brown hair that reached almost to her waist and somehow managed to make her school uniform look cool. He remembered thinking that her skirt must have been well more than the regulation two inches or so over the knee. And she had smelled nice. They'd smiled at each other most days and often left the library at the same time before going on their different routes home. Perhaps typical of his early forays into the world of male-female relationships, just as he was plucking up the courage to ask if she'd like to go out with him, she stopped coming. He wondered what had become of her. He'd never seen her since her library visits had ended. Probably she had been seen by a more confident, doubtless older, boy and hadn't realised the potential of the fourteen-year-old budding intellectual she had exchanged all those smiles with. So just one of a series of near-misses and maybes; strange how every decision, or lack of such, shaped one's future – he remembered having read somewhere that it was called the butterfly effect.

Almost twenty years on, and further along the Sussex coast in Chichester, the library there retained a similar feel and clientele; there were people filling time, or getting essays done, or finding out things as usual. He liked the way that the library staff were always helpful with whatever requests came their way; no doubt the stereotypes must have some basis in reality, but being earnest and interested in books didn't necessarily mean librarians were naturally boring people. Actually, there hadn't been a great deal of news to follow on that particular day. The political conference season was in full swing, with the Liberal Party reflecting on the consequences of having voted to form a pact of some kind with the new Social Democratic Party a couple of months previously. Mark doubted this would change the face of life or even politics in Britain too much and realised he didn't really care either way. He was more interested in reading a review of the cricket season in *The Times*. It had been an amazing summer of cricket, an Ashes series that England had won three one and it had been dominated by the re-emergence of Ian Botham. When Mark had been at Ford Prison in the mid-1970s, he had followed the rise of Botham – a real 'boy's own', heroic type of figure. Quite early in his career, and with high hopes of leading a new era for English cricket, he'd been given the captaincy of the national team. However things had not worked out and after a pretty disastrous twelve months or so he'd resigned as captain just after the second test of the summer series. Mike Brearley, a more cultured and erudite figure, had replaced him as captain and seemed to be able to bring the best out of Botham himself as well as the whole of the team. For the rest of the summer, Botham had performed miracles. England had been heading for a defeat in the third test at Leeds and with it the prospect of going two down in the series until he'd come in and turned the game around; then in the next Test match he'd bowled half the Australian side out for one run and again snatched a remarkable and improbable victory. Reading through the *Times* cricket correspondent John Woodcock's, typically masterful end of season review brought it all back. There really was nothing like test cricket and especially an Ashes series played out over a whole summer.

Meanwhile, he had to get back to the job at hand. As well as poisons, he needed to check out recent developments in criminal detection; no doubt things had moved on and he could do with finding out whether ricin and thallium were becoming any easier to detect. He had a large Chemistry encyclopaedia open in front of him, along with a couple of studies on the medicinal benefits and dangers of natural plants, illustrated with beautifully accurate drawings that betrayed the age of the books. Until recently publishers must have found it cheaper to include intricate, hand-drawn pictures rather than colour photos. The big advantage of public libraries was that you could work in them undisturbed; and if you didn't take anything out there was not even any record of what you'd been studying. Mark had forgotten the satisfaction, almost thrill, of covering one's tracks, of avoiding leaving any kind of trail.

He had heard about polonium and its alleged use by the Soviet secret service and had checked that out. Apparently it was a highly radioactive substance that made it an especially toxic poison. Although unlikely to be available through high street chemists, Mark thought it was worth a try at least. The beauty of it was that it didn't necessarily have to be taken orally: apparently it worked through touch. Botulinum toxin, used to treat spasms and migraines, was another possibility. It seemed likely that both would be rather tricky to get hold of, though, and certainly to do so without arousing suspicion. Better to stick to what he was used to. Mark had visited a good proportion of the chemists in and around Brighton when sorting out his in-laws last time. If he couldn't find what he needed around this part of Sussex, he reckoned he could always check out a couple of those who hadn't asked any questions last time and had appeared more than happy to oblige. Hopefully they'd still be trading.

There was something else which might prove useful. He'd picked up a brief comment on a documentary the other night about the discovery and formal recognition in America of a new and increasingly common illness that was killing gay men in different ways. Apparently it attacked the immune system and was pretty much untreatable. From what he had been able to find out, so far it had only been found in gay men, but he needed to get some more detail. It struck him that an incurable disease would be a brilliant change from his previous *modus operandi*, which could be useful should it come to any investigation in the future. However, and to be realistic, it was hardly likely that he could engineer it for

Gemma's mother to come into contact with an infected gay man, even if he was able to locate such a person in the first place.

It was almost four-thirty, and just as he'd done at their age, a couple of blazered school boys plonked their bags on a nearby table and pulled out their exercise books. Their arrival took Mark by surprise; the day had flown by and it was time for him to leave. He'd agreed to drive along to Littlehampton to meet Gemma after work at five. Before driving back to Petworth, they'd planned to have a drink and meal in a pub they knew near to her old apartment on the sea front.

Although he had made a few notes on this and that, it seemed that really not that much had changed in relation to poisons or forensics over the last few years. Perhaps he shouldn't have been surprised – it had only been just over half a decade, not long in terms of the history of crime and justice. He hurried along to his car: it would take a good half hour to get to Littlehampton at this time of day and, even though she was generally easy-going, one thing that Gemma hated was waiting around.

***

Gemma had walked down from her office in the town centre to Pier Road and the harbour. With the sun out, it was a pretty sight, in the slightly down-at-heel sort of way that perhaps best typified Littlehampton. There were a couple of fish and chip shops gearing up for the tea time trade, a Mr Whippy ice-cream van hoping to boost its takings for the day from the workers and schoolchildren straggling home to start their weekends, and a little late afternoon activity from the small group of fishing vessels – not enough to call a fleet, she reckoned. The mixture of noises and smells reminded her of family days out, mainly with her dad, come to think of it – the frying of chips, the generator from the ice cream van and the sound of the fishermen cleaning their equipment or hauling their catches up the harbour wall ladders and on to the walkway. The fishermen seemed to have had a decent day: there were plenty of flat fish, mullets and bass but also baskets of eels. Her probation colleague Mathew, the one who had taken over the supervision of Mark, was also a keen fisher and had explained at length to her that the River Arun was renowned as a habitat for those fish and had been so since Roman times. It hadn't worked as a seduction strategy but she had listened dutifully and learned, apparently by osmosis, a little about the different fish that lived in the area.

As was common practice on Fridays, Gemma had left work early and so was in good time. She sat on a bench across from the Arun View Inn and closed her eyes to the late afternoon sun, waiting for Mark to turn up as arranged. It was hotter than Gemma had thought and even merited some suntan lotion, on her face at least. As she rummaged through her bag for the familiar plastic blue bottle she noticed two seagulls fighting over the remains of an ice cream cornet, and being watched by a lone sparrow, on the off chance they'd leave something behind. Gemma had enjoyed her time in Littlehampton before the move to Petworth. There was no way she was going to live with her mother after her father died and the probation job that came along just as she completed her degree had had its moments, although she had never intended it to be long-term. She wondered if her dad had realised just how badly he'd been treated; but even if he had not, it was up to her to make amends. Gemma was sure he would have understood and supported her. She had to take it slowly, of course, but she was going to sort things, to get what she deserved and what she was sure her dad would be happy with, if there really was any chance he could ever actually know for himself. Even though it seemed to her highly improbable and to fly in the face of any logic, Gemma had never been able to quite dismiss the idea that there really might be life after death and she reckoned he would have been devastated if his daughter's inheritance was ever hijacked by some future step-father.

So far things had gone well enough. She was almost twenty-five, and could set a year or two as a rough target and the time to have it all worked out and through. The move to Petworth had paved the way for bringing Mark and her mother into contact; and she quite liked living with Mark anyway, he was pretty good company and not bad on the eye too; and so what if he wasn't long-term? She let the sun play on her eyelids. She wasn't a bad person, but her mother had been. It might seem like she was using Mark but she would make sure he got what he deserved too. Gemma knew she was never going to ride off into the sunset with Mark but she prided herself on being a fair person; if he helped her she'd be as generous as she could and she'd do her best to let him down gently when it came to it.

Recently she had become somewhat concerned that Mark hadn't settled into much since his release; and perhaps not surprisingly he appeared to be getting increasingly down about things and even a little insecure about their relationship. It wasn't an overly obvious or desperate neediness but his desire to please her was beginning to verge on the oppressive; she was thankful that at least he hadn't mentioned marriage. Anyway, she wasn't about to take responsibility for his emotional state. From her point of view they were partners in more ways than one and things were going along fine; after all, he was a grown up and knew there were no guarantees.

She heard a car pull in to the pub car park across from the harbour and hoped it was Mark. It had been good of him to drive her to work and a meal out was always nice. Although they hadn't got round to making any detailed plans, there was a sort of implicit agreement that Anne, her mother, had to be separated from her wealth one way or another and certainly before she had ensnared a second husband. Mark was pretty hopeless at keeping anything to himself and had let it slip that he was going to check out recent crime stories at the library. Mind you, she was surprised he was bothered about keeping anything to himself – surely he'd realised they were both thinking along the same lines. Perhaps being too obvious and brazen about things didn't seem right, or perhaps he just liked a little subterfuge for the sake of it – after all there was a kind of seductiveness to secrecy. Maybe tonight's meal would be the time to develop a proper plan of some type, to bring into the open what they had basically already agreed on.

***

Sure enough, it was Mark. She watched him lock the car and cross over to her bench.

'I haven't kept you waiting too long have I? The traffic out of Chichester was mad as usual.'

'No, that's fine, it's a lovely afternoon and I like it down here by the harbour. You know, I did actually quite enjoy living in Littlehampton; and we had some good times here, didn't we?'

They'd been regular visitors to the Arun View when they'd lived in Littlehampton and even though the menu was pretty limited and typical, the fish and chips was usually a safe bet and tasty enough, and Gemma went for that. They were on nodding terms with the landlord and Mark followed his advice and ordered the lamb cutlets, peas and chips followed by Black Forest gateau. There was no shortage of tables and they took their drinks over to one overlooking the harbour. Gemma got straight down to it.

'Well, did you find anything useful out?'

She needed to convince herself that Mark was on the same wavelength. He had spent the best part of six years locked up and, irrespective of whether or not it was possible to measure rehabilitation, that might have been enough to put anyone off risking going back again. Any such concern was soon allayed: if anything, he appeared to have assumed they had already started. He had clearly got over any compulsion he might have felt for avoiding spelling things out explicitly.

'Oh you guessed, did you? Yes, it was interesting I suppose, but really there's been little change since I sorted out Gordon and Jean. I did pick up a couple of ideas but not sure they'd be any better than the old castor beans made into ricin, along with a bit of thallium. Funny thing was, the only poisoning case I could find much of a report on was mine; it's strange, but I never really read the newspaper reports on it after I'd got sentenced. Actually I felt a bit of a celebrity and a bit weird too, reading about me without the people sitting around me knowing it was me, if you know what I mean.'

So there was no need to worry, he was big-headed enough to believe he could do it all again. Maybe that was a little unkind; she was glad he had enough self-confidence left. Even at this stage Gemma realised that while she would have to help Mark with some of the planning it would be better to keep as much distance as possible from any physical involvement, just in case things went wrong. She would have to make sure there was no hard evidence tying her in – no receipts, no finger prints – and she'd need that to make sure Mark had nothing he could hold over her if it ever came to it. At most she would have to ensure that any evidence was hearsay; and that it would just be Mark's word against hers. That was only if things went badly wrong of course, but there was no harm in imagining worst-case scenarios.

'Yes it must be strange, but you know, Mark, you're the expert, you can do this and you know I'll help as much as I can. We're in this together, remember that. So what do you reckon is the best approach, what worked best last time, and would it work again?'

This was more like it. Mark warmed to the task.

'Well, it's a matter of gradually wearing someone down, then upping the amounts when they're weakening. And it's important to get her doctor, or any doctor really, on side; get them to see that there is a gradual deterioration. What's on the death certificate is the key, really: that can avoid any detailed post-mortem or autopsy.'

She wasn't sure what it was, but it made her really quite aroused listening to him talk about her mother as some kind of subject. Mark was keen to explain his strategy.

'The first thing is to spend more time with her, to take her out and get her to drink more, to have meals with her when I can mix in this and that; to win her confidence, too.'

They'd finished eating and Gemma wanted to get him home while she felt in the mood. It made her feel better if she was treating him and letting him do what he looked as if he wanted to more than anything else. It offered a sort of equilibrium too, to balance her feeling that she was just using him.

'Okay, we'll invite her over to ours more often, and as you suggested you can take her up to London sometime and also help arrange a drinks evening or something at hers. You've got to charm her too; and another thing is to get that bloody Terry from the golf club out of her mind. He's been coaching her apparently and she sounded like she was enjoying it. I only picked up on it when I spoke to her the other day and she went on and on about him and her golf. I did ask her about that other chap, the one you said she'd met up with in Guildford, the one with the car, but like you said I think she's so full of herself that she's after someone younger. That should make things easier for you, I guess.'

She brought a bottle of red wine from the Arun View's fairly limited stock and suggested they get back home as quickly as they could. It was never too difficult to get the message across to Mark. It might seem a little calculating, mercenary even, but in her defence she had no intention of going with anyone else while they were working together, whatever might happen in the future. Anyway, she always enjoyed sex with him too.

As they reached home, their row of cottages looked as inviting as ever, nestled on the outskirts of Petworth and with a lovely view of farmland and the gently undulating Downs beyond. As Mark parked in the makeshift driveway at the side of their house, Gemma felt a wave of affection; he may not be her long-term plan, but why not enjoy things for the moment? It wasn't just about keeping him on track, it was about having a good time at the same time.

'Why don't you roll a joint while I get the glasses out?'

Mark didn't smoke much nowadays but he kept a little stash of Moroccan in case. Gemma had never been much into dope herself, but they liked an occasional joint and now seemed like a good time for one.

Mark didn't need much encouragement. They sat outside the back door. Old Mrs Mortimer in the middle terrace next door had no idea about pot and the Brays at the end were generally away at the weekends anyway, so there was no need to worry about the smell wafting across the back gardens.

Gemma poured them both second glasses and led Mark upstairs.

'Come on, we've got the rest of the weekend ahead of us and I think we should get down to some serious planning, this week has just about done it for me with probation. It really is becoming a shambles at the moment. Like I said, I'll keep it going for a few months but that's it. Let's arrange a do at my mother's for the end of the month while it's still fairly light in the evenings. Meanwhile, I've got my needs, you know.'

She let him undress her and sort her out, before doing the same for him and letting him finish off inside her.

Friday 25 September 1981

Over the last couple of weeks Mark had experienced increasingly regular feelings of *déjà vu*; perhaps surprisingly, they hadn't been particularly unpleasant and it was almost as if the last few years had been a mere distraction. They had decided on Saturday the 26th for the planned social evening at Gemma's family house in Farnham, and it had come around quickly. While Gemma had helped her mother with invites for some of the neighbours and a couple of recently acquired golfing friends and persuaded her to ask Ruth down for the night, Mark had been busy renewing his acquaintance with the world of plants and poisons.

Rather than visit the various and quite numerous chemists and supposed health shops he had previously used in the Brighton area, Mark had toured those in Chichester and then Portsmouth. Somehow it seemed more anonymous in larger towns and the further from Brighton the less chance he felt there'd be of him possibly being remembered. It was still easy enough to get castor beans which could form the staple and initial part of the plan; and producing powdered ricin from them was straightforward enough as well. Even though one of Agatha Christie's thrillers, *The Pale Horse*, had encouraged a wider awareness of the dangers of thallium, there were still heavy concentrations of it in the cockroach and rat poisons that chemists as well as hardware stores had plentiful stocks of. Mark had found it particularly useful in the past and although it was not completely untraceable, apart from a danger of hair loss it wasn't easily recognised, and after all the link with an early 1960s book by Agatha Christie wasn't an obvious connection to make. Come to think of it, a bit of appropriately targeted depilatory might not be such a bad thing in women of a certain age, he mused; and being realistic, it would take a fair while before any significant loss of hair would become apparent.

It had only taken Mark a bit of driving around to get more than enough of everything he supposed that he might need. The problem was that those shop-bought powders were more difficult to disguise than home-made ricin and would have to be used only as a last resort or a final push if needed. To begin with, apple pips and peach stones crushed up with ricin would be easy enough to slip into anything with a reasonably strong flavour of its own. Then he would need to make sure the right person, in other words Anne, was the only one whose food and drinks had the specially prepared extras included. Mind you, if there were the occasional slip up, one or two other guests suffering stomach cramps wouldn't be the end of the world; and there'd be no follow-up administering of regular doses with them, so any collateral damage would be limited. It would just be seen as a one-off complaint.

Although to a certain extent he was acting on autopilot Mark had realised that he was actually quite enjoying having something to work on, and some sort of direction and purpose at last. He had plenty of time on his hands and Gemma had encouraged him to drop in on her mother by himself sometimes as a way of getting things moving. In fact, he had called in for lunch last week with a ready prepared shepherd's pie as a first step and ostensibly to discuss the upcoming party. Gemma had helped by phoning her mum and telling her to give Elaine that day off; and Mark had prepared two separate versions of what had been his signature dish last time around and with his previous in-laws. The lunch trip had worked out well. Mark had persuaded Anne to open a bottle of wine and after a glass of that, along with her usual two or three cigarettes, any slightly odd flavouring was easy enough to put down to the special spices Mark hinted that he used with his cooking. He had decided not to hold back too much this time and even though he saw this as just an initial foray he had put a pretty hefty amount of ricin along with a dash of thallium into Anne's individual dish; he reckoned her taste buds would be pretty shot through anyway, given her less than healthy lifestyle. The military analogy seemed appropriate: he liked the way it smacked of a planned strategy.

They had sat out on the patio after eating and Mark had suggested he organise a trip up to London for a night out once they'd had the party. One of his old favourite bands, the Pretty Things, had a mid-week residency at the Marquee Club and he considered that a heavy night or two might help things along in due course. Mark would enjoying seeing the band again too, he had always liked their hard rock style and he promised Anne he would bring up his favourite album of theirs, 'SF Sorrow', next time he came.

Although he had managed well enough in terms of the conventional poisons Mark had made little headway in trying to get hold of any other drugs. He no longer had ready access to students and the student lifestyle. Since his conviction, he had lost contact with virtually all of his previous colleagues and on the one occasion he had visited the university campus where he had worked it was apparent he was not seen as a prodigal son, let alone a welcome guest. However, he knew one of his previous students-cum-suppliers, Greg, had gone on to take a PhD and might still be around the Brighton area. In the past Greg had always been able to get anything Mark had wanted; the problem was renewing contact. Strangely the only member of the Sociology Department who had shown any sympathy for Mark had been Craig, a new appointment who had only been there for a few weeks before his arrest. He reckoned it might be an idea to contact Craig and see if he knew anything about Greg and where he might be.

Anne had obviously enjoyed his visit and lapped up the compliments about her figure and sense of fun. He'd left promising her a good time the following weekend at her party and also that he would make sure he spent plenty of the evening with her. Even though that would be to take care of what she drunk and what it contained, he also felt a kind of almost charitable warmth toward her too. On his drive back to Petworth that afternoon it had struck Mark that loneliness was perhaps the worst of states to have thrust on you; and even if him helping alleviate that a little might not justify everything that followed, it did have some merit, surely. Anne had looked happy and whatever the motivations and outcome, he was sure that she would enjoy herself along the way. Maybe it was possible to rationalise everything; it might not quite be utilitarianism, perhaps more accurately what he recalled had been termed 'rational egoism' back in the late nineteenth century by some philosopher whose name escaped him.

Saturday 26 September 1981

It had all gone pretty smoothly and to be fair quite enjoyably too. Gemma was sitting on the back patio overlooking the garden with another glass of wine in her hand and feeling pleasantly out of it. It was approaching mid-night and Mark, Anne and two remaining guests, the neighbours from next door but one, had joined her and were enjoying the surprisingly mild late summer night. Two weeks since it was last full, there was only the slightest crescent of the waning moon apparent between the intermittent clouds that were drifting from right to left, slowly and noiselessly but also apparently purposely. Although the Seadons were retired and must have been approaching their seventies they had kept going as long as anyone and were telling Gemma's mother they had had their best night out for a very long time. As it had turned out there'd only been a dozen or so there – two more couples from Lynch Lane plus a couple of Anne's new golfing buddies along with their husbands – but everyone had appeared to enjoy themselves.

Gemma let the conversation and cigarette smoke drift over her. It had got to the stage of the analysing the guests who'd left and who were now being unpicked one by one – as loud, unsophisticated, boring, along with an occasional 'quite pleasant really'. She let them get on with it; after all, gossiping had always been her mother's favourite pastime. Seeing Mark in action had been something of an eye-opener for her; he really was a very smooth operator and Gemma could see things working out pretty much as she had hoped for.

She and Mark had arrived earlier that afternoon to get the nibbles and drinks ready. The idea of a buffet had appealed to Gemma's mum but it did leave a problem for Mark. In the end he had decided to leave the food un-tampered with as it would be too difficult to check who picked up what, and too many bouts of unexplained illnesses might have been awkward to explain. However, he had kept a close eye on Anne's drink. Somehow he had managed to spend virtually the whole night rarely wandering less than a few feet away from her, but also had never looked as if he was doing anything other than mingling and hosting. Gemma had made a point of watching him filling Anne's glass but even though she knew what he was up to she had only once caught him shielding the glass and fiddling in his jacket pocket for a little extra. Of course she was pretty sure that no one, not even her mother, knew about Mark's past. It had been over six years ago and there was no reason for anyone there or anywhere really to make the link. Gemma had never had the type of mother-daughter relationship that involved discussing boyfriends or partners. It had helped, too, that Anne had never shown the slightest interest in her daughter's work with criminals, aside from wondering why she even bothered to work at all. As far as Anne was concerned Mark was just a nice, articulate and attentive man who was her daughter's new and, given his charming manner, hopefully long-term boyfriend. She also liked it that he was a good deal older than Gemma: it helped develop a little empathy between herself and him.

Gemma and Mark had decided to stay over in Farnham as part of the plan and also because they were both well over any breathalyser limits. Mark had a thing about the morning after breakfast being a good opportunity to build on whatever he might have added to the drinks and food the night before; a fry up provided excellent camouflage for masking the bitter taste of ricin and thallium, while any odd tastes would be likely to be put down to the previous night's excesses. They even had a choice of rooms, too, as Ruth hadn't made it in the end. Her excuse had been a migraine but even though Anne was apparently her best friend it had hardly been unexpected – it was only on rare occasions that Ruth managed to get out of London and she seldom made any effort other than for herself.

Rousing herself from her reverie Gemma could see that her mother looked well the worse for wear; mind you, Mark had made sure she'd drunk plenty and given the mixtures he'd prepared her drawn look was hardly surprising, nor was the fact that she was complaining of a nagging stomach pain. The heavily applied make-up had worn off and what was left behind was less than impressive; maybe 'haggard' was a bit unkind but certainly 'gaunt' and 'faded' were appropriate descriptors. The top Anne had chosen for the previous night was too low cut. It hadn't been too obvious earlier on but by the end of the evening the revealing of protruding collar bones and below them a heavily furrowed décolletage was quite off-putting. The image in Gemma's mind resembled a re-working of Harry Beck's famous London underground map, with all the lines leading to increasingly emaciated breasts that were drooping at an alarming angle. Gemma realised how little she cared for her mother, and how much she resented her, and how much she wished things had been different; the posh house and all the trimmings couldn't make up for the lack of affection and love she had craved.

Eventually the Seadons had said their goodbyes and left. Mark had propelled her mother up to bed. In spite of her state, Gemma had heard her telling Mark that she had had a great night and, in a drunken slur, that he was too good for her daughter.

Gemma had called up to Mark: 'Let's have a last drink down here before we tidy up a little.'

She hoped he had thought to bring a joint or two; she'd never been a heavy smoker but sometimes it did just feel right. He didn't disappoint and he seemed full of himself as well.

'Well, I think that's started things; if we hang around and prepare her breakfast then we can leave it for a week or two and work out a timetable. Do you fancy a little smoke before we go to bed?'

Gemma beckoned him over and put her arms round him.

'You were great, Mark, and I was hoping you'd have a joint ready. We – well, really you – deserve it.'

Tuesday 6 October 1981

Since the evening at her mother's Gemma had found it increasingly difficult to keep a focus on the day job. The driving to and from Littlehampton, the paperwork, the interminable hanging around at various courts, the hopeless and hapless offenders, and alongside all of that the idiots she had to work with – it had never been how she had envisaged her life panning out; and she was determined that it couldn't go on for much longer. Seeing how Mark had taken to his new, really renewed, role had made her realise that it could be for real; things could work out the way she had occasionally imagined. Although Gemma had never had a clear or detailed plan in mind, she could see herself getting her revenge, and her dad's, and perhaps a good deal more besides. Meanwhile, she knew she had to keep everything else as normal as possible, to carry on as the supposedly dedicated junior probation office keen to make her way in a chosen profession. She realised she had to keep herself above any future suspicion, to keep up the image, just in case. That didn't mean she couldn't help keep Mark on track and help with the practical side of things, too.

Now that it was all out in the open between them, a good deal of their time was spent discussing progress and strategies. It had given Mark and her a closeness which Gemma was enjoying more than she had thought and which he seemed pretty happy with too. Maybe it was the thrill of danger, the allure of engaging in something which was so beyond the bounds, so callous and calculating too; it was little surprise that crime could be so addictive. They had agreed the do at Anne's had been a good start and that Mark's approach of regular and varied doses was the only way to make it all seem natural. She had been amused by the fantasy he'd told her he'd had after his previous efforts with his in-laws: essentially it involved him being given the sobriquet of 'The Cocktail Murderer' and being accorded similar notoriety to the most infamous of villains. Gemma wondered if he really believed a place in history beckoned.

As it was, and for the next stage of things, Mark wanted to add to the mix by getting hold of some more conventional but illegal drugs before the promised night out in London with Anne. He had arranged to meet up with his former colleague Craig later in the week to see if Craig could help him make contact with that market. Meanwhile Gemma was pursuing an idea she had about one of her current clients, Roger, which she reckoned could potentially add an extra element to Mark's cocktail approach. Knowing she had an official appointment with Roger scheduled for later that day had given her a little more enthusiasm for the drive down to work that morning.

It was surprisingly warm for early October and she had put on a low cut strap dress and ankle sandals, and more lipstick than she usually wore for the office. She felt good and knew she looked good. She had always been well aware of her ability to manipulate older males. Typically pervy, in spite of his pro-feminist posturing and self-righteousness, Mathew hadn't been able to lift his eyes as far as her neck when she had breezed into the office earlier; and her boss Gregory had been embarrassingly but quaintly incoherent when he'd hovered around her desk, seemingly with some memo which he'd never even got to deliver. Even Lizzie told her that she looked summery and full of life.

She was reading through Roger's file with more care than she would normally have done when the internal phone buzzed and Lizzie spoke.

'There's Roger here to see you, Gemma.'

'Thanks, send him in please.'

Roger must have been in his late forties if not older, judging from the details he'd provided as part of his mitigation when he was sentenced at the local magistrates' court a few weeks back. Apparently he had been conscripted for his two year's national service from 1949. An army background, even from some time ago, usually helped impress magistrates and he had been lucky to be given a two-year suspended sentence for cultivation of marijuana, which he had claimed was for personal use even though there was enough to last him a couple of lifetimes at least. Tall and thin, with piercing blue eyes, he looked like, and probably was given his offence, an ex-hippy as well as ex-soldier. One of the conditions of his suspended sentence was that he would be supervised by a probation officer and that task had fallen to Gemma.

The bell on her office door tinkled as Roger pushed it open; he did a double-take.

'Bloody hell Miss, you look good; makes these visits a real pleasure, you know.'

Gemma had taken to him on her first contact immediately after the court case, not for any particular reason other than that he was more articulate and easier to talk to than most of her clients. And to be fair, with those eyes, he reminded her of Peter O'Toole, which wasn't a bad comparative. She decided to get straight on with her ploy. She never doubted he would fancy her anyway. As with so many local cases, probation and police officers, court staff and local solicitors generally knew one another, had established decent working relations and were happy to share information. In this case, Gemma had managed to read up more than usual on Roger's background from his solicitor's unofficial notes. As well as the army background he had held a variety of jobs including farm work and as a crew hand on a fishing trawler; he had lived on what appeared to be some sort of small holding for many years and apparently was a keen naturalist. It was just an inkling of an idea but Gemma remembered one or two of the supposedly cooler students at her university had either found or bought magic mushrooms; these were apparently quite common and, as well as giving a decent buzz, were also potentially poisonous, or at least might be mistaken for mushrooms which were.

'Look Roger, we both know you're not going to change your habits of a lifetime but that with some care and common sense you'll probably not get in trouble again. However, you'll have to at least consider other ways of enjoying yourself. You don't have to break the law, you know; and you know I'll have to write regular reports on how you're doing for the next two years. So you will have to be straight with me right from the start.'

She decided to trust her instincts and push on.

'I shouldn't be saying this but I've read up on your situation and personally I don't mind what you get up to or what you find when you're out and about in the countryside, but it would be wise not to grow anything you shouldn't at your own place, that would be asking for trouble. You do realise that your suspended sentence can easily be revoked and you could actually end up in prison?'

Roger seemed to see what she was getting at. Either she had been too obvious or it was something he was already more than familiar with: probably the latter, she fancied.

'It's a fair point, and you know, funny you should say that, because there are lots of natural things you can find that are just as good as dope and not illegal either.

You may be surprised to know that I'm pretty clued up on all sorts of different plants and even mushrooms and I know where the best places to find them are. And if they grow in the wild, what could be more natural?'

She wasn't surprised; her instincts were usually never that far out.

'You shouldn't really be telling me, Roger, but I'm glad we're being honest. We need to be if we're going to get your supervision right. And you know, I'd like to think that I'm not just your probation officer.'

For a moment Gemma wondered if she'd gone too far. Maybe she should play it reasonably straight for now, or strike a balance at least. She needn't have worried; Roger was warming to her plan without realising it was one.

'Come on Miss – actually, can I call you Gemma? I know that's your name. As I said, these things aren't illegal, they can be dangerous but I know what's what in that area. And you know, it's really nice and even therapeutic foraging in nice woodlands, I often go to the New Forest, it's beautiful down there. And come to think of it, you're right, there's no need to risk growing things in my own back yard, that would be stupid.'

This was going to be easier than she'd thought or expected.

'Well, as we're going to be meeting up for a couple of years and as I do want us to have an honest working relationship, you can call me Gemma if you like, but only when there's just the two of us, of course.'

She carried on.

'And yes I agree the New Forest is amazing, even if I don't know it as well as you, I love it too.'

Roger was clearly in his element.

'Look, I know we've got to be professional and everything but you're not working all the time, why don't I take you down to some of my favourite spots sometime?'

Gemma was well aware it was straying well beyond the professional, but then she had no intention of being professional for that much longer anyway. Nonetheless, she knew that she had to be the one pulling the strings. Feed them the ideas and then let them imagine they were the ones in charge – that was how it was with Mark too.

'Well, I'll see Roger, but you know, it might be a nice change. The thing is, it might put me in a compromising position, though.'

Roger was hooked and Gemma realised she'd have to make sure he wasn't expecting too much, and also she'd have to deal with Mark's jealousy, but it would be great if she could get hold of some pretty deadly mushrooms. And so what if Roger fancied her? He wasn't too bad looking in a weather-worn kind of way and to be fair a bit of flirting wouldn't be too unpleasant. Oddly enough, and somewhat tangentially, she remembered reading something about a new religious cult or sect, the Children of God she thought, which encouraged female members to flirt with potential recruits as a way of getting them involved – something like 'flirty-fishing' it had been called.

Meanwhile Roger was well away with planning it.

'There's loads of fly agaric around, they're like the magic mushrooms, you know, but better, and then there's some to avoid, death cap in particular. The thing with amanita mushrooms, which is what they are, is the slight differences that you have to be aware of. Also how to prepare and cook them, they're ten times more poisonous if eaten raw, you know.'

'Well, it would be interesting, Roger, and fun too. I'll see when I'm free and maybe in the next week or so and we can coincide it with our next session. I've got another meeting to go to now so let's arrange that next session, maybe two weeks today?'

'Sure Gemma, that sounds nice, but you know October's a good month, the best really, before it gets too cold. Next week would be good, better in fact. Maybe we could bring the next meeting forward a little?'

Gemma didn't want to look too keen but that made sense and the sooner she got something the sooner she could help Mark to push on with things.

'Well yes maybe, let me check a couple of dates and get back to you, I've got your phone number here. And, Roger, just a nice trip out into the countryside: nothing else, Ok?'

'Sure thing, Miss, or Gemma if I may. I understand and you can trust me, I'm not a grass or anything, this would never go any further.'

Although it wasn't just that she had been alluding to, she believed him. He actually did seem to be a genuinely nice man, if slightly unconventional.

Thursday 8 October 1981

Turning into the university grounds, Mark tried to fight the somewhat surprising feelings of regret, almost sadness, that had been building up as he circuited Hove and then Brighton on the A27. As he pulled off the Lewes Road and up to the university campus the rich autumnal colours hiding the not unpleasant 1960s buildings reminded him of how it could have worked out. Designed by Sir Basil Spence, Sussex University certainly put to shame the functional technical colleges that Mark had tried his luck at earlier in the year.

It was strange but after less than a year his time in prison had become a kind of blur. 'Doing time' was such an accurate description and he'd never really dwelt on what might have been in terms of his academic career – he'd focused his frustrations and anger more on how Justine and others had let him down. He would surely have been a Senior Lecturer, if not Professor, by now.

It was just after 4 o'clock; various classes and lectures must have just finished, judging by the groups of students heading to the bus stops or car park. Mark realised that it was probably the first week of teaching after the summer break so it was not surprising there were so many around. He remembered how attendance gradually declined as the academic year progressed and students found more interesting things to do with their time. The initial keenness and naivety of the quaintly-named 'freshers' soon receded, particularly when it was clear that attendance at lectures wasn't monitored in the ways they might have been used to at school, and indeed that such events were in many ways peripheral to student life anyway.

From what he'd picked up the social sciences were still attracting more and more students and no doubt the Sociology department was thriving. Craig was waiting for him outside the science block: he didn't drive and Mark had offered to pick him up and go into town for a bite to eat and a couple of drinks. Craig was the only person there whom Mark had kept in touch with and they had decided it wouldn't be a good idea for Mark to risk bumping into any of his ex-colleagues, and particularly Sandra. She'd been his friend and mentor when he had started at Sussex; in fact their relationship had strayed beyond the professional but in the end her suspicions, coupled with jealousy when Justine took over his attention, had helped everything unravel back in 1974.

'It's good of you to invite me down, Craig. Let's go to the Ship for some food and then maybe the King and Queens, I haven't been there for years.'

Brighton was still his favourite town and it felt good to be back there and to drive down past the entrances to Stanmer and Moulscomb parks, then along Lewes Road and through the outskirts of town, on to Victoria Gardens, the Old Steine fountain and the Royal Pavilion. They parked just off Church Street and walked through the pavilion grounds, resplendent with purple and pink hydrangeas still in full bloom, then past the front of the ornate, Regency-style Theatre Royal and on to the Old Ship Hotel. A few office workers were grabbing a quick drink after work but it was easy enough to find a table overlooking the promenade and Palace Pier.

Craig filled him in on what had been going on in the world of Sociology. He had only just started in the department at Sussex the term before Mark's confession and subsequent imprisonment, but had been the only one to offer any kind of support or sympathy; and the only one who had visited him during his years away. Sure, there might have been a bit of ghoulish interest, and it did fit in with his interest in developing the sociology of deviance courses he'd taken over, but it was better than the way just about everyone else he had worked with had lined up to condemn him. He even suggested he could try to help Mark get back into his old role.

'You know I could have a word with Michael, he's still Head of Department, we're bloody short staffed right now and they're looking for part-time people, hourly paid.'

It was nice of Craig to suggest but Mark knew it would never happen.

'That's nice of you Craig, but they'd never have me back either at Sussex – or anywhere else, for that matter. These places might try and appear liberal and unprejudiced but a conviction for murder would be a step too far. Anyway I've got plans of my own, you know.'

He didn't want to give too much away but needed to see if Craig could help.

'The thing is, I've basically lost touch with people I used to get stuff from and I could do with getting some drugs, speed or coke maybe; just for me and Gemma, old habits die hard and all that. I know you're into that and there were a couple of students who used to help me out in that direction, one in particular was Greg Corner and I think he was planning to go on to a PhD in our department. I was wondering if you knew anything about him or had any other contacts?'

'Bloody hell Mark, I'm not really in touch with it all, but I do know who you mean and he actually completed a year or two back; but the thing is, I never really knew him anyway. I do get a bit of dope from time to time but that's about it and not so often now. I reckon I'm getting past it but I suppose I could try and ask around surreptitiously.'

'Fair enough and that'd be nice, but Greg could get hold of all sorts. Anyway, it was worth a try, I guess. We could go to the King and Queens but I guess that'd be a bid dodgy just trying to score randomly.'

The look on Craig's face indicated that he agreed.

'Yes I don't think that'd be a good idea – you never know if any of our students are there – but let's go and have a pint anyway.'

It had turned out to be a pleasant enough evening. Mark enjoyed picking up on a bit of gossip and had learned that there had been something of a division in his old department. On the one hand there was a loose combination of the Marxist and feminist advocates who seemed to think their purpose there was to convert the undergraduates who came their way to the fight for justice; and then there were those tending to support a more qualitative and broadly interpretivist approach, who were pretty much focused on research for the sake of it. As well as that there was Ernest, close to retirement but still number-crunching and seemingly in a world of his own. By virtue of longevity, really, Ernest had been given the title of Reader and Deputy Head of Department and was the only one there interested in quantitative research. According to Craig, Michael had been promoted to Professor and had been trying to keep it all on track while busy building a mini-empire there. It was all quite interesting but not much help to Mark, or to his and Gemma's plans. He dropped Craig off at the house he'd bought close to the Seven Dials and they promised to keep in touch, but Mark doubted Sociology would play much part in his own future.

Wednesday 14 October 1981

Gemma had dropped Roger off at his rented cottage in the little village of Tortington, on the outskirts of Littlehampton and just up the road from Ford prison. It really did merit the title of small holding and beyond the quite impressively stocked vegetable patch there must have been close on an acre of open countryside that came with the property. She didn't bother to ask where he had been cultivating his marijuana; probably better for her to keep some professional distance.

All in all, it had been quite a successful day and she had a bag of fly agaric mushrooms along with a handful of *Amanita phalloides*, better known as death cap mushrooms. Driving home through Arundel she was looking forward to getting back and providing Mark with something useful. He'd been a bit down since his unsuccessful trip to Brighton and she needed him to keep positive and busy.

She had met Roger late that morning at the Littlehampton office for his regular supervision meeting and then taken the afternoon off so they could get to the New Forest for some foraging as Roger put it. To avoid any gossip, she hadn't told her colleagues and rather than leave the office together they had met up on her way out of town; the slightly cloak and dagger approach had appealed to Roger. The afternoon itself had turned out to be great fun; it had taken her back to school trips out to local woods, nature reserves and the like. Roger had told her to bring decent walking boots or something sturdy at least and he was dressed for the part: a warm jacket with plenty of pockets, brown cord trousers and what looked like mountaineering boots. He looked quite good and certainly good for his age; fringed with his slightly greying but full head of hair, his face evidenced the warm, slightly careworn, look of someone who was happy in his own company. She'd been a little taken aback when he told her he was almost 52. It was nice that he obviously fancied her and took every opportunity to help her over gates and through the various bits of woodland they visited; and especially that there wasn't anything obviously salacious or creepy about his concern for her. She was surprised that she had found herself thinking that maybe when this is all over she could keep in touch with him. If he had actually made a move she wondered whether she would have put up that much resistance – she reckoned it was those blue eyes that did it.

It had soon become clear that Roger was something of an expert. On the drive out of Sussex, past Portsmouth and over the mouth of the Solent he had lectured Gemma about the ins and outs of mushroom hunting. He was particularly excited as September to November was apparently the best time of year, and even more so today because the rain they had had overnight would trigger the appearance of mushrooms as well as improve their chances of finding what they wanted. On top of all of that, she had learned that the New Forest was probably the most fruitful place in the country for such fungi hunting.

Once they'd passed Totton and parked up they had started on a route that Roger obviously knew well. As they moved from one wooded area to another, he had explained why the wicker basket he'd brought was ideal as it held the mushrooms but at the same time let the spores through the gaps in the rushwork as they walked. Roger had various brown paper bags in his pockets to separate out different batches; he explained that plastic bags were no good as they made the mushrooms sweat and spoil. When they had found a cluster of fly agaric in a small copse of what he told her were ancient beech trees, he'd stopped Gemma just pulling them out by hand and showed her how to use a knife to cut them from the base. He explained that fly agaric were not the same as liberty cup mushrooms, which were the type known colloquially as magic mushrooms, but reckoned they were stronger and had a nicer effect as well. Even though she had felt like a schoolchild he hadn't talked down to her and she had really quite enjoyed his attention; he'd even brought a separate knife for her to use as well. What she'd liked most, though, had been the magnifying glass he had fished out from somewhere to inspect each of the mushrooms they located. If he had added a deerstalker it wouldn't have been out of place. After a couple of hours, as well as the fly agaric and death caps which she had told him she wanted as a sort of souvenir – and which Roger seemed to show little concern over her interest in, so enthused was he by having a pupil to collect with – they had also harvested a decent supply of edible varieties, particularly chanterelles and blewits, which he assured her would be fine to cook and eat.

By early evening Gemma had arrived back in Petworth in good spirits and the rest of the night had turned out pretty well too. Mark was made up he had another and different ingredient to add to his collection and repertoire; and he seemed pleased that she was getting involved too. She didn't bother to mention how much she had enjoyed spending the time with Roger – no point in tempting fate, or more precisely jealousy. Even though he had claimed to have taken most available drugs during his student days, Mark had never tried mushrooms and had suggested they try a small amount of the fly agarics she had brought back, as they weren't the deadly ones and so as to check them out, as he put it. He had dried a couple out and made some tea with them and they'd certainly worked. Gemma had never taken acid but Mark had compared the effect to a mild trip; everything gave the impression of being softer and somehow fuzzier and Gemma had felt light-headed and excited at the same time. They'd sat out in the garden till the early hours and had just listened to the sounds of the countryside. It was either karma or just luck, but there was a full moon that night and the fields behind their cottage had been lit with an ethereal glow that enhanced the whole experience. In the end she hadn't got to sleep till around four or five and had had to phone in sick the next day; even though there was no particular hangover she was tired and just couldn't be bothered.

Tuesday 27 October 1981

Mark was preparing a decent selection of ingredients from his supply of castor beans, fruit pips and stones and thallium. As well as all of that, he thought he might as well try out the death caps for the first time too.

It was the day he had arranged to take Anne up to London for a night out and he knew that they needed to get on with sorting things out. Gemma was clearly fed up with her probation job. In fact, of late she seemed to be pretty fed up in general. The only things she had shown any enthusiasm about recently revolved around the guy who'd got the mushrooms for her and was on some kind of probation register, apparently for growing marijuana – mind you, he did sound an interesting character. Mark put aside a definite twinge of jealousy – Gemma had told him he was fifty-two, after all. They had been discussing how to hurry things along with her mother the other night and Gemma had made it clear that she wanted to get on with it and to have enough money to do what she wanted, and in the not too distant future as well. It had struck him at the time and he didn't know if it was just because he hadn't noticed it before, but Gemma had been looking really good recently. She'd started swimming a couple of evenings a week, driving the ten miles or so up to the public pool at Haslemere; and she'd taken to wearing tight t-shirts or jumpers over jeans, all of which highlighted her great figure. She was a good few years younger than him and looked it, and he realised he'd need to make sure he kept her happy and, as she reminded him from time to time, well off.

They had only been up to Farnham a couple of times since the soiree-cum-party, just over a month ago now and time was beginning to drag. On each occasion Mark had done the cooking and added a little of his favourite flavouring, ricin made from castor beans; but now was the time to really go for it. After all, it had taken a good few weeks to wear Jean, his previous mother-in-law, down and she had definitely been in a worse general state of body and mind than Anne before he had begun the process.

Mark had set off for Farnham early that afternoon. Gemma had helped to persuade her mother it would be good for her to get out and that it would be a nice opportunity for her and Mark to get to know one another. Also that Gemma would be happy to have some time to herself while they were away – which wasn't a lie. She had always liked to have her own space, to use that irritating description, but since they'd moved in together, and with Mark not working, she'd rarely had any time without him being there, and it was beginning to do more than just niggle her. Once the date had been agreed Anne had arranged for her and Mark to stay over at her friend Ruth's flat, just off Oxford Street; Mark had suggested that it would be too late to get back after going to see some live music at the Marquee and they might as well make a night of it. He'd even prepared a couple of versions of his signature shepherd's pie in the usual separate individual casserole dishes, one with edible mushrooms added, the other an additional sprinkling of fly agaric and death's cap. Only a small amount the first time: he needed to monitor the results to begin with. It'd be too obvious if he overdid it. Mind you, he had done a bit of research and discovered that poisoning from mushrooms was a pretty common occurrence. Of course, it might be easy enough to recognise at autopsy but he reckoned the symptoms could easily be confused with a bout of gastroenteritis.

As he drove into Farnham and on to Lynch Lane he wondered if this was his real identity, and destiny too. The slightly disarming thing was that it all seemed so normal. The back door was unlocked and Mark went straight in; he found Anne in her usual spot in the living room. After checking that the housekeeper, Edith, had left for the day he suggested they eat something there before taking the train up to Waterloo.

'Good idea to line our stomachs, Anne. I fancy a few drinks and a good night out later.'

Anne looked quite presentable, at first glance anyway. The heavily applied make-up had done a reasonable job in hiding the stretched skin and deepest wrinkles and her trouser suit over a high-necked blouse hid the bony chest and protruding collar bones. He had never been able to understand the obsession so many women seemed to have for developing a gaunt and emaciated, almost cadaverous, look. It was something to blame the sixties for and certainly didn't do anything for

Mark. After all Marilyn Monroe's shoulder blades and clavicles had been well hidden, as were those of Rita Hayworth, Lana Turner and the Hollywood icons of earlier decades; and it was curvaceous females who inspired the classic paintings of Rubens and Rembrandt, and before them the Renaissance masters such as Titian and Correggio. Anyway, all that was by the by. He pulled up a chair and launched into action.

'You look well Anne, and the trouser suit's very nice.'

Anne smiled at him.

'You know it's good of you to take time out for me, Mark. I'm going to make sure I have a good time. I've been having odd stomach pains and cramps recently and I'm fed up with just sitting around feeling my age.'

That sounded positive, and as if the previously administered bits and pieces of ricin and the rest were beginning to have the expected cumulative effect. Mark realised it would be useful to get any deterioration in Anne's health logged by her doctor, and as soon as possible.

'Well no harm in seeing your doctor about that, it's important to get things checked out, we'll make an appointment when we get back, you must remind me. Anyway, let me heat up the shepherd's pie I've brought and we'll get going after. I thought I'd take the car up to the station, park it there and leave it for the night. You know, I'm looking forward to it too: I haven't been to London for a while now. It'll be a pleasure – and you do look bloody good, by the way.'

He parked up just after half five and they settled into their seats on the train. Mark got himself a beer and Anne a gin and tonic; it might help take the edge off any pain or stomach cramps from the mushrooms. He watched the suburbs of South East London flash by: Woking, Weybridge, Walton-on-Thames and Surbiton. He really was quite good at this – older women certainly took to him, and not just older ones, he'd like to think. Waterloo station was heaving with commuters going the opposite way to them; they battled through to the underground and took the tube up to Bond Street. It was a short walk to Ruth's and they picked up the key she had left for her flat from the downstairs neighbour. Apparently, she was out for the afternoon and probably wouldn't get to see them before tomorrow morning if they were back too late that night.

'Let's get ourselves settled in at Ruth's first then we'll head up to Wardour Street and the Marquee in a bit, it's just a couple of stops on the Central Line up to Tottenham Court Road and then just round the corner.'

***

As Mark and Anne emerged from the tube into the London night there was an unmistakable air of anticipation as the Soho area was beginning to spring to life. They walked a short way up Oxford Street before turning down Dean Street and cutting through to the Marquee part way down Wardour Street. They picked up their tickets at the door and Mark ushered Anne to a table as near to the back of the club as he could find; although it was pretty dark inside he still felt a little uncomfortable and obvious, as if he was either a gigolo or else reduced to having to take his mother out for company. He wasn't going to overdo things but intended to get Anne reasonably drunk and to add some of the thallium he'd acquired to her drinks whenever he could. Fortunately thallium salt was still easy enough to get from most chemists; although best known as a rat poison it was still widely used to treat skin infections such as ringworm. The big advantage was that its effects didn't become noticeable for at least a week or so; however, one of its known side effects was hair loss and he didn't want to risk raising any suspicions too soon. He had only brought about half a teaspoon's worth with him and knew he had to be careful; apparently a gram was close to a fatal dose. His plan was to add a little to a couple of drinks and then a bit more when he prepared breakfast, or coffee at least, the next morning at Ruth's. Mark had been trying to get hold of some polonium which he'd found out had been the cause of a number of deaths by poisoning in the 1960s, particularly at laboratories in Israel, and which was just about untraceable, but had had no luck so far. The two chemists he had tried had given him rather odd looks when he'd enquired about it – it was obviously a long shot.

The band that night were doing the usual sound checks as Mark returned from the bar with a double G & T and a Southern Comfort; after all, he might as well enjoy himself too or at least try to take the edge off things. He had chosen that particular night because the Pretty Things were scheduled to be playing but, annoyingly, there'd apparently been a late change. He hadn't bothered to check the tickets at the door and only found out at the bar. He passed the news on to Anne.

'According to the barman there's been a change to the bill. The Pretty Things have cancelled, he didn't know why, but Marillion are a new band who played their first gig here last week, as a support act, but because they were so good they've been invited straight back. They're progressive rock with a bit of jazz thrown in apparently. Should be worth hearing, I'm sure.'

All of that meant little to Anne, of course, and he was pleased to see that she looked as if she was enjoying herself.

'Thanks Mark, it's been a while since I heard any live music. They do look very young, I must say, and so do most of the crowd.'

Mark could see that was the case, he tried to play it down.

'Well they do to me too, I guess it's inevitable but I have seen a few other older people in the audience as well. Come on, drink up and I'll get another one in before they start.'

Mark had noticed a group of what looked like students rolling joints at a nearby table and the atmosphere in the club was already exhibiting the distinctive sweet aroma of pot, mingling with that of cigarettes, sweat and alcohol. He wondered about trying to get something for himself to help the evening along but thought better of it. From what he'd picked up from Anne over their recent meetings she was pretty much against drugs of the illegal variety and there was no point in antagonising her. Regular dope wouldn't help much with the plan anyway.

As it turned out the music was great and Marillion were certainly worth watching. Given the reason he was there, it felt a little ironic that Anne had slipped him a ten pound note which was more than enough for the drinks and entry. He had kept the G & Ts flowing and had no trouble adding the extra ingredients he'd brought along. By the end of the set Anne was well away. They'd even got to their feet and swayed around a bit for the last couple of songs; although Mark had made sure they didn't venture too far away from their table.

As they left and hit the night air. Mark hailed them a cab rather than try to battle with the tube again. It was only a few minutes down Oxford Street. Things had gone as well as Mark could have hoped. Anne was clearly quite taken with him and a few more weeks, perhaps more realistically months, and maybe Gemma and he would have sorted it all out.

By the time he had manoeuvred her out of the cab and up the two flights of stairs to Ruth's apartment, Anne was too far gone for a night cap. He'd finish off the thallium in the morning.

'You get a good night's sleep and we'll leave after we've had some breakfast tomorrow morning.'

At least she didn't try to kiss him.

'Yes that was great Mark, I've had such a good night. Gemma's a lucky girl to have someone like you. My Jeffrey wasn't much fun you know... nothing like you. I think he just had no idea how to treat me, really.'

He chaperoned her into the spare room and let her drift off. Ruth's bedroom door was closed but she had left him some bedding on the sofa. Even though it doubled as a bed Mark was happy enough to sleep on it as it was. As he'd promised he phoned Gemma to tell her how it had all gone and to suggest they follow things up by regular weekend visits to Farnham. You had to keep the momentum up; he'd learnt that much last time.

Saturday 5 December 1981

Mark brought the tray back with the leftovers of breakfast on it into the kitchen where Gemma was tidying up and making her own breakfast. He poured himself a glass of orange juice. It was Saturday so Edith wasn't around, much to Gemma's relief. They'd driven up to Farnham the previous tea-time. Mark had prepared individual dishes again and they made sure Anne had eaten the one with the rather wider selection of mushrooms in it. Their plan had been to stay over and spend the evening encouraging her to have a few drinks with them, duly prepared by Mark. Anne had just about managed to get the hang of the video recorder and they'd watched two episodes of her current favourite drama, *Brideshead Revisited*, while Mark plied her with as much G & T plus additions as he could.

'She looks pretty bad this morning, she's only had half the coffee and hasn't touched her toast. I think we'd better call Dr Ferguson again.'

Gemma agreed. 'Okay, will do, I reckon he's getting the picture so I'm sure he'll come. I'll go up and tell her to stay in bed for the time being.'

'Look, Gemma I think this could be all over soon, I recognise the signs. Are you definite you want her out of the way? She is your mother.'

Over the last few weeks, Mark had harboured the odd doubts as to whether Gemma was really determined to go through with things. He needed to reassure himself that it was a joint effort and he wouldn't be left by himself to take any kind of blame. It all felt a little strange working with someone rather than alone. Of course, Gemma had played her part and come to think of it had really planned the whole thing, but, apart from the mushrooms, it was he who had got hold of the various poisons, mixed the drinks and prepared all the food.

'I've said this all along, Mark, we're in this together. I can never forgive her, you know that, I'm fine with things. The sooner the better, in fact.'

Mark put the doubts to the back of his mind.

'The thing is, I've got to make sure there's no link to my past, and that no one makes that connection. You're sure Anne has no idea about how you met me or about my past? And what about your work colleagues, did you ever let anything slip?'

Gemma did her best to reassure him.

'No, I've never told my mum anything about that, or about anything really, she's never been that interested anyway. It's only a few people at work, maybe Mathew, David and Lizzie who obviously knew about your past, but I've been distancing myself from them recently and in any case there's really no need for them to find out anything about my mum when it happens. I've never really talked about my family to any of them. Also, I'm planning to hand in my notice before Christmas, in fact I've decided that I'm going to next week. I've been thinking about it and I've got a few more days leave to take so if I hand in my notice next Tuesday my last day should be the twenty-second which will take me to the end of the year, so I'll be out of it before anything happens anyway.'

Yes, he was probably being a little paranoid. There was a slight danger that someone might make a link if Anne's death was reported in any detail and if they remembered the press reports around his trial back in the early 1970s. However, that wouldn't be likely to happen if Anne's death was just seen as natural causes; and there was no one he felt he had to confess to this time. Actually, there was no reason why it shouldn't be easy enough to keep things quiet, as long as they got it right. One elderly widow dying of natural causes in Farnham was hardly likely to make the news in Littlehampton, or anywhere else for that matter.

Since Mark's trip to London, each weekend they had made a point of either visiting Farnham and staying over for a night or else bringing Anne to stay with them in Petworth. Mark had added smallish amounts of deaths cap mushrooms, along with concoctions of ricin, thallium and crushed peach stones, to their, or rather her, evening meals and they had made sure Anne drank enough to mask any discomfort. It had been a strain having her around and having to encourage her to drink and smoke, but if anything Mark felt it had brought him and Gemma closer together, having a common goal and aim. And it was clear to see a general deterioration in Anne's health. She looked thinner and greyer and complained of an almost constant stomach pain. It was strange but it eased Mark's conscience that she also said she was having a great time and apparently felt years younger spending time with them. He had insisted they take Anne out drinking on a few of the weekend visits and she had obviously really enjoyed herself too. He'd said to Gemma it made it easier for him to rationalise things, to think there was something positive amidst the overall destruction, really. It had been the same with his mother-in-law years ago: seeing her enjoy herself had helped provided some kind of balance in his mind. He had always believed that it was all a case of equilibrium – short-term enjoyment, even hedonism, against long-term drudgery; quality versus quantity. For some reason, and somewhat elliptically, he mused that Pete Townshend had written that he hoped to die before he got old back in 1966, even if he was pushing middle age now and still going strong.

***

Dr Ferguson arrived shortly before lunch. Even though it was a Saturday he'd been at the surgery sorting through the usual backlog of paper work and prescriptions and offered to call on his way home. He'd become the family's doctor soon after Anne and Jeffrey set up house in Farnham in the late 'fifties and had been a particular friend of Jeffrey's before his death. Gemma remembered him calling around when she'd caught the usual round of childhood illnesses. In particular, she recalled his horn-rimmed glasses and her father sitting by her bed as the doctor moved the cold metal disc on the end of his stethoscope and listened to whatever was happening inside of her – the sound of her heart and lungs, she was told. He had looked old to her then, even though it had been his first practice, and she reckoned he must be well into his sixties now. Gemma greeted him with affection and told him to go straight up to her mother's room. She said she'd have a cup of tea ready for him when he'd finished.

Dr Ferguson smiled at her reassuringly.

'I know your mother's not a well woman, Gemma, and she does herself no favours with her drinking and smoking, you know. And don't you worry, you can call me whenever you need, after all your family are just about my most longstanding patients.'

As far as Mark could tell this was just about the ideal scenario. Dr Ferguson was unlikely to have kept himself bang up to date and from what he could tell probably had less sympathy for Anne than he would have had for Gemma's father, or for Gemma herself. Also, as he'd been working by himself in the practice for years he wasn't likely to have close contacts, or indeed any, with the doctors who had tended Mark's in-laws in Brighton more than seven years ago now.

'He's great Gemma, just right, in fact. He'll probably point to a generally unhealthy lifestyle and I can hint at some possibilities to him which might help when he has to do the death certificate.'

Gemma put the kettle on and opened a packet of biscuits, knowing the doctor would be happy for a natter. He came down after little more than ten minutes and deposited his medical bag on the table, a battered tan brown, soft leather affair that appeared to Gemma to be the same one he had brought to her bedroom when she had her bouts of measles or mumps years ago. He offered his prognosis.

'Well, it could be a number of things, but she's her own worst enemy. I even had to stop her having a cigarette when I was up there. Anyway, I think it could be a touch of pneumonia, possibly even something I've been reading up on called bronchopneumonia, so I'll do you a prescription for penicillin.'

Mark couldn't help himself.

'Well we've been looking after her every weekend, but we've also taken her out and encouraged her to have a drink or two, just to see her enjoy herself. I hope that's okay?'

'I know, you two have been wonderful and it's not your fault that Anne is the way she is, and there's no harm in a few drinks as far as I'm concerned. In fact, she said how much she had enjoyed having you around recently. Actually, in these situations I have often found that the patient's mental state is just as important as the physical, if not more so.'

This was exactly the sort of doctor they wanted.

'Well, I was doing some reading, up doctor, and I was wondering if there might be a touch of hepatitis there too, affecting her liver maybe?'

Dr Ferguson absent-mindedly dipped a digestive into his cup of tea and nodded.

'Um yes, not impossible, but there's not much available for treating hepatitis as far as I know.'

Mark pushed on.

'Yes, I heard that too and you're right, apparently only steroids, or corticosteroids I think they're called. Look, I hope you don't mind me interfering?'

'No, there's no harm in you taking an interest and I'll bear that in mind too. I must admit that it's difficult to keep up with everything and run a busy practice at the same time. You know, it's funny but after being a doctor here for many years I've come to the conclusion that there's often nothing much wrong with most of my patients apart from the fact they're getting old.'

They saw Dr Ferguson to his car – just as Mark would have expected, a leather-seated Rover 3500. Gemma managed to put on her best tearful expression and gave him a hug.

He rolled down the window as he left.

'Now you call me whenever you need, and don't worry, none of us is getting any younger.'

They walked back round the side of the house and into the kitchen.

'He's brilliant, just the kind of doctor we need.'

Gemma agreed.

'And he's a really sweetie too, he'd never believe we could be the cause. Maybe we should really get on with things now.'

That was just what Mark wanted to hear. He couldn't quite believe how smoothly things seemed to be going; he felt almost apart from himself and what was happening, on a sort of roll. His excitement was almost palpable and the words came pouring out.

'Yes, good idea, let's get her down for lunch and I'll add in a decent quantity of the castor beans. I found out last time that ricin is very difficult to detect anyway. Then she can come up to ours next weekend and maybe we can sort it all out for good around Christmas. I reckon ricin and maybe those mushroom bits you've got will help and I'll add in some thallium as well. You know thallium is the best, it's pretty common and the salt has no taste or colour or smell and is bloody difficult to detect because it seems to affect a few different parts of you simultaneously. Just about a gram would be enough to finish off someone in Anne's condition and another good point is that it wouldn't work straight away, could take maybe two or three days, Like I said, from what I can find out it's very difficult to detect. Dr Ferguson would have no chance, we can hint at some suitable cause, I'll look up a few possibilities next week.'

His obvious excitement took Gemma a little by surprise, even though it was exactly what she wanted too – Mark going for it and taking over. It was quite disturbing in some ways, the ease with which she'd got him to return to the very behaviour that had supposedly ruined his career and wasted six-plus years of his life. It gave her a definite sense of power too; and he had no idea that for her this was the start of things, the start of a new life which she had no intention of him being a part of. It wasn't that she was going to abandon him altogether, she would make sure he got what he deserved for helping her out and meanwhile there was no harm in having some fun together. Gemma had always been pretty single-minded in terms of what she wanted and needed to do and when. Sure, she could play the part of lover, partner or accomplice and play it well, but that was all, a temporary necessity; it might even be pleasant enough but not forever. It wasn't hatred or anything like that – just that she'd had enough of that part of her life. She wanted him to be happy too, but just not necessarily with her.

'Yes good thinking, Mark. Let's get her to spend next weekend at ours and we can come and stay here over

Christmas and try to get it all finished then. There's lots of room here and you're right, the week between Christmas and New Year would be ideal. Dr Ferguson will be happy to get things done quickly and without too many questions, and so will the funeral people too.'

Gemma put her arms around Mark and kissed him.

'I do fancy you when you take charge and spell out how you're going to sort everything out. Let's get back home after lunch, we don't need to spend two nights here. We'll make sure my mother's comfy and I'll leave her some sandwiches for tea. You can do what you want with me then.'

She hoped that, when it came down to it, letting him down gently might work but realistically was hardly confident it would. In fact, the way Mark had been recently, rather too needy and going on about their future together, she knew that was an absurdly optimistic expectation. Still, one thing at a time.

Wednesday 6 January 1982

It had been a long day and quite a stressful last couple of weeks but as Gemma poured a final drink for herself and Mark, whisky for him and a glass of wine for her, she felt a glow of something akin to satisfaction. Everything had gone so smoothly and basically just as they had intended. The funeral that morning had been a very low-key affair: firstly a service at the crematorium in Aldershot, the nearest to Farnham, and then a small gathering at the family house in Lynch Lane. Ruth had come down from London along with a couple who had known Anne and Jeffrey when he had worked at the Cunard office in London. They had stayed until early evening. Dr Ferguson had come, along with his wife, there had been two of Anne's golfing friends and a few of the neighbours who'd got to know Anne since the party there last September. And of course, and seemingly more upset than anyone, Edith, along with her husband. That had been a surprise to Gemma as she had never seen or even heard mention of a husband, but Alfred turned out to be a surprisingly chirpy character who insisted on telling everyone how her mother had depended on Edith for just about everything. Her uncle's partner Joseph had sent a condolence card from Spain but had been too ill to travel.

Gemma pulled her armchair over to the French windows, next to Mark, and looked out over the patio and lawn and to the fruit trees beyond.

'I'll be glad to get rid of this house, it deserves to have someone living here who appreciates it. You know, I always dreamt of being part of a big family here, I even had an imaginary one when I was younger. It's a shame to say but it was never the place it should have been for me, or my dad, and probably not for Mother either. I wonder how long it will all take to sort out.'

Mark reached across and put his hand on her arm.

'I think that's probably for the best. Yes, it is a lovely place and maybe does deserve better; we've done what we planned and it's time to move on. I can't believe how well it's worked out; as well as the house, you've just got the odds and ends from the will to deal with and it'll all be over. I'll organise selling off any bits and pieces worth anything. And you've sorted your job out as well so don't have to worry about that anymore.'

Gemma was pretty confident that the will and her legacy would be no problem. When Jeffrey was ill he and her mother had prepared a will that left everything to Anne herself and then, if and when she should die, to Gemma. There were no complications and no additions, she was sure of that; her mother probably had no intention of dying when it was drawn up. It had been useful that after her father died, over four years ago now, his side of the family had had virtually no contact with Anne or Gemma since then. As well as that Anne herself had been an only child and had no family left apart from Gemma. Anyway she knew it wasn't going to be anything like in those films and plays where everyone gathered in the living room while the will was read out to the accompaniment of knowing looks, nods and groans; and with the finger of suspicion pointing directly to the main beneficiary.

'Well I'm going to see the family's solicitors next week, they're based in South Street right in the centre of town and have been there for ages apparently. I phoned them and spoke to one of the directors I think, he said he'd actually known Jeffrey quite well and that he couldn't foresee any problems; and I'm the executor as well, which is fine apparently. It'll just take a few weeks to finalise details about her assets and do the paperwork and then we can put this place on the market.'

They sat back and listened to the rain splattering on the patio and outdoor table and chairs. Their feelings of relief, satisfaction almost, were tempered with a difficult to explain air of gloom. Mark broke the silence.

'This might be our last night up here, it'll be nice to get back to Petworth. We seem to have been away for ages and it's been a bloody strain at times, but it's worked out fine. Are you sure you're okay with everything, Gemma? You must feel a bit weird.'

'Yes, of course; you've sorted it all out brilliantly.'

Gemma asked Mark to light her a cigarette; she let the events of the past few days play back in her mind. She didn't feel anything like remorse, she had done what she had felt was right, she had done it for herself and for her dad too.

***

Anne had died on Tuesday 29th December. Mark and Gemma had stayed over in Farnham for Christmas Day and Boxing Day and had made sure they had had plenty of heavy meals and lots to drink. In spite of the real reason for them being there it had been quite fun in a bizarrely black sort of way and Anne had obviously really enjoyed herself. Gemma had been quite happy to see that but it had no impact on her resolve; it was almost as if they were giving her mother one last hurrah and somehow it seemed to have made everything kind of easier. She could see what Mark had meant when he'd said it provided a weird form of rationalisation for it all.

Mark had stuck to his plan of adding a sizeable, and as it transpired fatal, amount of thallium salt to the Boxing Day dinner and they had gone back home on the Sunday afternoon. Just as they were getting ready to drive back on the Tuesday morning to see how she was, and to see if the thallium had done its business, Edith had phoned them in an evidently distressed state and said she couldn't get Anne out of bed and feared the worse. Gemma had put her foot down and they got there within forty minutes and sure enough Anne was clearly dead and had been for a few hours at least.

Gemma had calmed Edith down as best she could and Mark called Dr Ferguson. He had come round straightaway and after examining Anne had signed the medical certificate and put down the cause as respiratory failure as a result of bronchopneumonia. It seemed a bit of a mish-mash of an explanation to Mark but he wasn't about to complain. Dr Ferguson said how sorry he was but that it was perhaps not unexpected and told them to register the death at the Farnham register office and to get at least a couple of copies of the death certificate. Gemma had done that the next day and there'd been no comment when she'd said that they wanted the funeral as soon as practicable.

It certainly seemed to help that it all happened in the Christmas and New Year holiday period; it appeared as if everyone just wanted to move things along and to get on with a new year. The local funeral directors had called in with remarkable efficiency early on the Wednesday morning and it had all been planned and arranged with relatively little fuss. They were even able to fit in the funeral for the following week, particularly as Gemma said her mother had specified she didn't want to be buried and a cremation was what they had agreed on. Edith had been more upset than anyone and Gemma resolved to make sure she gave her something when the will was finalised, maybe one or two of the vases as a keepsake and a few hundred pounds too.

PART THREE: AUTUMN 1982

Sunday 19 September 1982

'You can't let him drag you down, Gemma, you've got to be your own woman. Surely now you don't need to stay stuck out in the middle of nowhere. Why don't you come and live up here in town? We'd have a great time; you could really go for it now. You're an independent woman, after all.'

Rebecca had been one of the few school friends Gemma had kept in touch with even though they had seen little of one another since doing their A-levels at Farnham Girls Grammar School back in 1975. At that time, Rebecca and Gemma, along with a few carefully chosen others, had considered themselves as the 'in-crowd' at school – pretty well off, good looking and knowing it. They were the ones who had older boyfriends with access to cars. It was little surprise that since then she had developed a persona that was a kind of cross between a second wave feminist and an upper class debutante. They were sitting outside the Crown in Princedale Road, Holland Park, along with Victoria, who had been the Head Girl at Farnham in their final year. Although she had never been particularly close to Victoria, Rebecca had met up with her by chance when she'd been browsing the various boutiques and vintage clothing shops in Ladbroke Grove earlier in the summer. They'd gone for a coffee and cake at one of the trendy little cafés there and found out that, without having realised it before, they both worked for the BBC at Shepherd's Bush, just the next tube stop down the Central Line from Holland Park. After catching up on the last few years, they had agreed to meet up during their lunch breaks whenever they could. It hadn't been long before Victoria suggested Rebecca move into the apartment on Norland Square which her father had bought a few years previously as an investment. Rebecca had leapt at the opportunity.

In their mid-twenties, living in the increasingly fashionable Notting Hill Gate to Holland Park area and with fancy-sounding titles for what was effectively secretarial work at the BBC, it had worked out nicely for both of them. They were keen to impress on Gemma the advantages of what they clearly felt was their current and cool lifestyle; and to be fair, it had certainly struck a chord with Gemma. Over the last few months, really since packing in her job with the probation service the previous December, Gemma had been getting more and more bored with life in Petworth. As she had planned, Gemma had given in her notice and left the office in Littlehampton not long before her mother, Anne, had been sorted. It was strange that neither she nor Mark ever really referred to themselves as murderers or killers and just seemed to see themselves as arrangers, expediters even, although passing it off as some form of involuntary euthanasia might be stretching a point.

Initially she had been kept busy, dealing with the will, the valuation of the house in Farnham, encouraging

Mark to sell off whatever he could from the family's belongings and all the attendant paperwork. There had been a period of almost basking in the after-glow of success and revenge and she and Mark had even had some quite pleasant times together. However, she hadn't changed her resolve that she and Mark were never going to be forever. Since early summer, really, the lack of change and direction had been preying on her mind and she'd been getting increasingly tetchy. It struck her as ironic that as she tried to make it clear to Mark that she wanted to do more with her life he seemed to be ever more content with their lifestyle and to have become more clingy than usual – it was as if her trying to distance herself had the opposite effect on him.

The thing was that without work, and without any really close friends, she was finding him more and more irritating. Fair enough, he'd been great, he'd done what she, and they, had wanted but that was it for her. Some nice times together and reasonable sex weren't enough for her, but whenever she mentioned wanting to do more by herself she could sense Mark's panic and desperation almost, and she hadn't bothered to pursue things. And then, to cap it all, last week he had even asked her if she wanted to marry him when she'd told him she was planning to go away for this weekend. The thing was that she wasn't sure if Mark's behaviour might not be a kind of camouflage, anyway; a part of her didn't or couldn't believe that he was quite as contented with life as he made out. He had taken to going to the local pub by himself and kept harping on about her lack of affection – by which he meant sexual interest, of course. Perhaps the message was getting across to him;

but either way she knew she had to do something different with her life. It was in desperation almost that she had looked up and contacted her old friend Rebecca, a few weeks back now. Rebecca had told her that she and Victoria had met up and were living together and that they'd love to see Gemma. They had arranged for her to come up to stay for the weekend; and she was enjoying herself in a way she hadn't for some while.

Although the Crown was still very much a local pub it was beginning to move slightly upmarket along with that part of West London in general. They were enjoying a pretty decent bottle of Mateus Rosé and the brief splash of an Indian summer, which certainly complemented one another. It was warm enough for them to be wearing crop tops over the designer jeans they'd picked up yesterday afternoon on a shopping trip down the King's Road in Chelsea.

Gemma had come up to London on the Friday afternoon and the three of them had gone to see the widely acclaimed revival of *Guys and Dolls* at the National Theatre that night. After their Saturday afternoon shopping expedition, last night they had gone to town in more ways than one. Victoria, whose family seemed to be pretty well connected, was a member of the swanky Annabel's nightclub in Berkeley Square and had booked the three of them in. She had helped persuade Gemma to buy a loose, flowy, knee-length dress in cream for the occasion from Peter Jones up by Sloane Square, along with some fancy, high-heeled, red sandal shoes. Gemma had never spent so much on her clothes but, as she told herself, she'd never been such a rich woman as now and she might as well get used to it.

The evening had been a great success: Annabel's had been packed with what was obviously a very wealthy crowd but even so the three of them had attracted more than their fair share of attention. They'd hardly had to buy a drink all night and then had been driven back to the flat by someone who appeared to be a cross between chauffeur and dogsbody of the City banker who'd spent a couple of hours trying to get Gemma to go back to his own apartment with him, before doing the decent thing and seeing them all home for the price of her phone number and a kiss on the cheek.

Like Rebecca, Victoria was delighted to catch up with another old school friend and also with the prospect of having some different people to hang around with. She was full of herself; clearly in her element at being the one who'd brought the three of them all together and organised their weekend activities.

'We were bloody amazing last night; and you, Gemma, that Simon, he couldn't take his eyes off you and had made sure he'd got your number. And those other two guys who sent the bottle of champagne over, did you see the looks we were getting. My God, Rebecca's right, you've just got to come and live up here. Why not buy somewhere yourself? Like you said the other day, you've got your own money. I mean, I know I've got Daddy's but that's not same as your own.'

It certainly sounded pretty tempting but then there was Mark. Gemma's plan had been to extricate herself from Mark soon after her mother's death but dealing with her family's estate and selling the house in Farnham had taken longer than she had envisioned and they were still together, and, unless she had misread him, as far as Mark seemed to imagine, were pretty much a permanent fixture.

Even though she never intended for her and Mark to be forever, and even though she had basically used him to get things sorted out, Gemma did feel a twinge of guilt as well. She and Mark had been together for getting on for two years now and to be fair they had had their moments. It was always an option that they could do what Mark plainly wanted and settle down with enough money to live more than comfortably for as long as they wished. The thing was that she wanted something more, or at least different. It wasn't just the weekend in London; she couldn't help feeling that he held her back, that what he wanted was fine for him but not for her. To put a more positive spin on it, she didn't think it was the best thing for Mark anyway; he might go on about how pleased he was with things, but he wasn't the type to sit back and just take it easy. He might be a good deal older than her but he was still only in his mid-thirties.

Enjoying the wine and sun, Gemma was flattered and excited that Victoria and Rebecca were so keen on her moving up to London.

'Yes I suppose I could, the thing is Mark. He assumes we're going to stay together and I didn't tell you this, he even asked me to marry him the other day when I told him I was coming up here. Typically desperate, really. I'm not sure he really meant it but the thing is I do feel bad about it.'

Rebecca and Victoria couldn't contain themselves. Rebecca started.

'Oh Gemma, like I just said, he'll drag you down, you know that, you've said so yourself. You must put yourself first.'

Victoria chipped in.

'Yes, and you've told us you don't really love him anyway. Look, he might be a nice guy, I'm sure he is, but you can't spend your life with him just because of that. You know you'll have more fun up here with us around.'

She paused to let Gemma think before pushing on.

'Look ,why don't you stay tonight as well? There's no rush for you to get back to Sussex, is there? We could go and eat at the Belvedere – it's brilliant, it's some sort of seventeenth-century mansion apparently, on Abbotsbury Road. Daddy knows the manager or something and the food's meant to be amazing. We can talk it through, it always helps to get things out into the open and to have someone who'll listen. You can stay with Rebecca and me whenever you want while you're getting everything fixed.'

Gemma realised they were just being honest and she knew they were trying to help and were right too; of course, what they didn't know was that she and Mark had planned and carried through the murder of her mother and that she had to be pretty careful with how she handled him. She had been assiduous in making sure that there was no direct evidence linking her to her mother's death: she'd bought none of the poisons, except the mushrooms, of course, but there were no receipts involved there, and she knew she could manage Roger easily enough if she had to. As well as that, given Mark's previous record, she had more than enough on him to ensure it would be straightforward enough to put all the blame and guilt on him should it come to it. She was well aware that, logically, if it came down to his word against hers there would only be one winner, but nonetheless she was also well aware that he could at the very least make life more than a little awkward for her. As well as that, though, she did acknowledge that Mark had helped her avenge her father's death and life and she never intended to be unfair to him, or to hurt him unnecessarily. She would try her best to let him down as gently as possible. Anyway, that was all a little beside the point for now: why not stay another night? She was beginning to like London and could see herself having a future here.

'Yes that would be nice, if the two of you are sure you don't mind me staying another night. And I know you're right, I fancy doing something different and I know I can't stay with him as well. Basically I like him but that's all. It'd be good to have a chat tonight and I'll do my best to clear things up with Mark when I'm back in Petworth.'

***

Looking back, it had been a long nine months. Finalising the details of her legacy had taken most of the year so far and had been a long-winded and tedious process. Gemma's solicitors, a well-established local Farnham practice, had assured her that there were no obvious issues and that it would be basically straightforward; on that basis she had let them take over managing the probate. Things hadn't moved that quickly, however; it had taken a couple of months before she had even got the grant of representation, as it was called. After that there'd been a lot of organising, advertising and selling to do. It was amazing quite how much her parents had stocked up in, after all, only around twenty-five years. The house itself had attracted a fair bit of interest when they'd put it on the market in late March and there had been a sort of bidding war before it was sold by the end of May for slightly above the initial asking price of £120,000. The real bonus, though, had been the paintings and furniture. Mark had been careful to get everything properly valued and they had resisted selling the whole lot as one deal, in spite of the various offers to 'take the lot' from antique dealers in Guildford as well as Farnham. She had to admit that he had done a really good job and had been right to insist on selling everything individually, either through the 'buy and sell' adverts in local papers or at auction. The Parrish paintings had been the high spot and they'd got almost £30,000 for the two of them, along with another £3000 for the unattributed oil painting plus good prices for the various watercolours. Then the Victorian furniture and numerous other decorations and vases had got decent prices too. On top of that there were the shares and savings that her mother had been left after her own father and uncle had died. That had been the real surprise, the icing on the cake as far as Gemma was concerned. Both her grandfather and great uncle had bought substantial shares in the Cunard company between the 1930s and '50s, which had passed to Anne and now on to Gemma herself. This gave her a few thousand shares, making her one of the larger private shareholders in the company.

140

Even though she wasn't one hundred per cent sure about their motives, Gemma had taken the solicitors' advice and decided to leave the shares untouched for the moment. As it was, after their fees and a few other expenses, she was left with well over £160,000 plus a guaranteed basic, index-linked income of twelve thousand a year from the family's investments, without even touching the share capital.

Monday 27 September 1982

The crunching of car wheels on the gravel path at the side of the house followed by the opening and slamming of doors jolted Gemma back to life. She'd had the afternoon to herself and after a desultory bit of tidying up had spent the last hour or so with a glass of wine, which had only been refilled once so far, idly flicking through the latest edition of *Cosmopolitan* while waiting for Mark to get back from his latest trawl around the antique dealers in town. Maybe the wine was to give a little Dutch courage, but that, along with the tediously liberal and open-minded responses to readers' issues and problems – Gemma was sure they must be made up by the supposed agony aunts – had helped her drift into a pleasant, late afternoon reverie.

To be fair, Mark had worked hard and been pretty successful in getting rid of virtually all her mother's bits and pieces and for very good prices too. He had really thrown himself into planning for their future and she did feel guilty; however, today had really brought it home to her, she'd spent too long just treading water and pottering around. It was over nine months since she had given up her probation work and getting on for a couple of months since the family's money had finally been sorted. Apart from what she had set aside for getting herself somewhere to live when she left Mark, it was all settled in the joint account they had opened after buying their own house and for the time being had decided to use for Gemma's legacy.

She knew she had to tell Mark she'd had enough and wanted to move on; even though she hated that hackneyed expression it best described just what she wanted to do. The fact that she hadn't actually cheated on him made Gemma feel better about it all. And it wasn't as if she hadn't had the opportunity. Apart from the occasion in London when she'd stayed with Victoria and Rebecca, she had seen Roger, her mushroom man, again, even though she was not involved in any official, probation-related, way with him anymore. She'd told Mark she was tying up a few loose ends in Littlehampton and had let him take her on a couple more foraging missions in the New Forest, this time to relieve her boredom and purely for pleasure. They'd had a really nice time; autumn in the New Forest was a special time and for a few hours the stresses of the last few months had faded. It had been about a year since their first foraging trip and it felt strangely comforting to be back. Roger had smelt good too, a nice earthy aroma; and the fact that she knew for sure there was no way he would play any part in her future gave her a sort of exoneration. She'd let him kiss her and explore her a little too; when two of his fingers slipped easily inside her she almost gave in but something had stopped her going any further. Maybe a kind of loyalty to Mark; even though she knew they had no future she didn't feel right doing anything until she'd actually told him that. It hadn't helped that Mark seemed absolutely incapable of taking any kind of hint.

Since getting back from London a week ago, Gemma had been putting off confronting Mark with her need to move away and on. Somewhat forlornly she had hoped he might arrive at the same decision but she needed to stop kidding herself and get on with things. It hadn't helped that the last few months had not been too bad, and it wasn't as if they'd had a particularly bad or awkward week either. In fact the last weekend had been quite pleasant, they'd been to the cinema in Chichester to catch Richard Gere and Debra Winger in *An Officer and a Gentleman* on the Friday and had a nice meal out and a good few drinks on Saturday. Mark had been more than attentive and as usual there had been plenty of sex, but she knew she was stringing Mark along and even though she didn't think his proposal of marriage was really serious, she knew he was waiting for an answer; something which she'd promised him would be soon.

Staying with Rebecca and Victoria had really just confirmed what Gemma had been thinking about her life and future. She wanted to live a bit, to meet different people and London seemed as good a place as any to do it; even from that brief experience she felt she'd fit in and be part of something. It wasn't that she had any definite plan, just a feeling, a certainty really, that she deserved a good time and that she had the resources to do so, alongside a nagging and growing belief that Mark was holding her back. It wasn't necessarily or even the case that she felt she could do better, but just that Mark was never intended to have been long-term. That provided some sort of rationale if not justification; and even without the London trip she knew for sure that she wouldn't be short of offers either. After all, even though she wasn't particularly interested in him, Simon, who had homed in on her at Annabel's on her first visit, had followed up his interest and already phoned her a couple of times, luckily when Mark was out and about. Initially he'd invited her to see Genesis at the Hammersmith Odeon on this coming Thursday; apparently he had some of the best tickets in the place. When she had said she couldn't make that he'd asked if she would ever consider letting him take her out and her 'maybe' had led to a second call, the next day, this time asking if she'd like to see AC/DC with him on the last of three concerts they were doing in mid-October, and again at the Hammersmith Odeon. He'd told her that he also had backstage passes for that gig and Gemma didn't see why she should say no. Sure, he might be rather full of himself, and even a bit smarmy, but he ticked a few boxes: he was nice enough, very well off and must have some pretty decent contacts. From what she could gather he was one of a new breed of City traders, who were becoming known as 'yuppies', young upwardly mobile professionals or something like that, apparently after they'd been dubbed with that title by some American journalist. Anyway, why not let him be the start of her new life? And by then she intended to have tidied things up with Mark as well. Although she had resisted going any further with Roger and could hardly fault Mark as a lover, Gemma was definitely starting to fancy the idea of having sex with someone different.

Once she had made the decision to take up Simon's offer Gemma had rung Rebecca to ask if she could stay over that weekend, for the gig on Saturday the 16 October, and was met with screams of delight. Victoria had phoned her the next day and said she'd keep an eye out for flats in their area for her to look at. Even if they were a bit full on, it felt nice to be wanted.

As Mark came in, Gemma got up and put the kettle on. She let him tell her about the day he'd had and the price he'd got for the last couple of side chairs they had to sell, then launched into it.

'Why don't you sit down Mark? I've got something to say. I know you've been waiting patiently and I'm really grateful for all you've done but I'm not ready to marry you or to stay here with you either. There's things I want to do and I want to, I need to, do them by myself.'

Maybe it hadn't come out exactly as planned but it had come out. It had probably taken less than ten seconds to blurt it out but by the end Mark's whole demeanour was transformed; he had slumped back in his chair and seemed shell-shocked. She felt she owed him a proper explanation and was conscious it was in danger of coming out all wrong.

'It was lovely of you to want to marry me and I've never been asked before and I have thought hard about it, I promise. And it's been great being with you since you got out from Ford but I've just had enough living here. I gave up the probation job ages ago and I want to do something different now. I've being getting more and more bored and it's not fair on you either. Look, I know it sounds glib but I want to move on, to do something different with my life.'

Mark went to the fridge and opened a beer. He appeared calm enough but she could sense his tenseness and knew there'd be a blow up soon. He came back into the front room but didn't sit down again; he grabbed the top of the chair with some force, as if to keep himself in one place.

'What is it you want to do, then, and why can't we do it together?'

His voice sounded unnaturally strained and perhaps an octave higher than usual.

'Well, firstly I'm going to move to London, I've got friends there and there's just so much more to get involved with as well. I need a change, Mark.'

She could see Mark's mood turning from shock to anger as he processed it all.

'It's those bloody upper class snobs you stayed with the other weekend isn't it? They reckon you could do better than being with me.'

While that might not be too far off the mark, Gemma was well aware that it wouldn't help to bring anyone else in to the explanation.

'That's not it Mark, I've been thinking about this for months now.'

She knew it sounded trite but couldn't help herself.

'It's not about you, you've been great, it's nothing to do with anyone, it's about me.'

Gemma didn't know how she had actually imagined this would play out but it seemed as if it was all going on outside of herself. It was like watching a scene from a play or even a soap opera. It was all so stereotypical, just as one would script it. She wondered if Mark was actually going to hit her. She could see his anger fighting against his panic.

Mark was trying to keep a lid on things, he knew that losing his cool wouldn't help especially if there was any chance of rescuing things – the thing was he was bloody angry.

'You've just used me, you've got what you wanted and that's it. You've been planning this all along and now you think you can just say thanks and goodbye, well no bloody chance, that's not going to happen.'

Gemma realised that she needed to try to calm him down.

'That's not the case, Mark, it's just I don't want the same as you, not now anyway. And I know you've helped me so much and I'm not going to leave you with nothing and walk away, I never would.'

Gemma wondered if it was time to offer him some sort of deal. The thing was that the way he was responding, she doubted it would make things any easier. She could almost hear his brain cranking into the next gear.

'I can see it now, you've played me along. For all I know you've got your eye on someone else and always have had. I bloody trusted you and I love you.'

Why did it always come down to that, why did he have to believe there had to be another man involved? Okay, Simon was on the horizon, but Gemma knew that he was merely a side-effect and certainly was not the cause. She tried to explain but knew that at this stage it wouldn't help that much.

'Look there's no one else, there never has been, I just want something else, something different. I'm not going to rip you off either, I wouldn't do that after you helped avenge my father for me. For a start, I'm going to pay off the mortgage on this place and then sign it over to you one hundred per cent, and I'll give you half the money from the furniture you've sold, that'll be a good few thousand too.'

It was obvious Mark was hardly listening anymore; and certainly wasn't interested in working out a deal or pay off. Perhaps not unexpectedly, he went on the offensive.

'So you think you can just buy me off then? I'm not some kind of hired killer, you know; and anyway I've got enough on you to ruin you. It was you who wanted to get rid of your mother, after all; it was all your idea anyway.'

Gemma knew she'd have to ride things out for the time being but she was pretty certain that once he thought about the money and house he might calm down a little. After all, they weren't married anyway and had been together for less than two years. In fact she was being more than generous when she thought about it. She decided it best not to point out that she was in a much better position to ruin him than the other way around; or that she had made absolutely sure that all the hard evidence, not to mention his impressive criminal record, would make it easy enough for her to have him put away for life again, and with little chance of an early release this time around.

She tried to pacify him.

'Mark, we could both do that to each other, but when you've thought about it you'll realise we can both do well enough from all of this. We can be sensible about things. I just don't feel the same way about you as you do about me, but that's life.'

At least she avoided saying that they could still be friends.

Mark grabbed another beer and went out to the garden. She heard him start his car up and reverse aggressively out on to the lane. He somehow managed to make his Escort sound in pain. That had been another source of his frustration too; an ageing Ford economy car hardly suited his self-image and didn't match up to her sports car. Anyway, him letting off steam was probably for the best, she thought; he could think it all through by himself. Mark wasn't the type to do anything stupid, she knew him well enough. He'd like her to think he was going to make some massive gesture but would probably just go and have a few drinks at their local and feel sorry for himself. She poured herself a glass of wine and felt an odd sense of relief, almost a glow. That was the worst of it over. No doubt he'd sulk around for ages and even come back and plead with her for them to stay together; but once that had failed she reckoned that he'd probably try and get as much as he could from her, and that might make it all the easier to handle. For a moment Gemma wondered if she really did know him quite as well as she thought; and if there was perhaps something she might not have taken account of. She couldn't be bothered to dwell on that at the moment, though.

Gemma knew there was no going back – it had been what people called an epiphanous moment. The sense of unburdening felt quite overwhelming and a part of her wanted to tell someone, Rebecca perhaps, but she resisted calling her, out of an odd sense of loyalty almost, as if the moment was hers and shouldn't be shared just yet at least. There'd be plenty of time to let her friends know and to get on with the practicalities of moving away.

Wednesday 20 October 1982

The last few weeks had been awkward. Mark had been in a deep sulk and Gemma had tried to be matter of fact about it. He'd had a real go the other evening, accusing her of abandoning him and, with over three million unemployed, plus his criminal record, bemoaning the fact that he would hardly be able to present himself as a top prospect to future employers. She'd done her best to convince him that he'd be fine by himself, he'd soon find someone else and that he could sell what would soon be his house in Petworth and then have enough to start off anywhere he fancied.

Of course, she did feel a little guilty; after all, she had used him to help sort things out and to pay her mother back and help draw a line under her father's death, but then she had made sure he had done well enough from it all too. Bloody hell, she had even let him have sex with her a couple of times over the last few days. He'd always been a bit shallow in that respect and anyway that wasn't the reason she didn't want to stay with him. Now she just wanted to make sure that the move to London and the start of her new life went as smoothly as possible. Things had moved pretty quickly in that respect and, with a bit of luck, she'd have the flat she was in the process of buying finalised within a few weeks and certainly by the end of November at the latest. To keep him reasonably happy and acknowledging his hubristic tendencies, she'd promised Mark they'd keep in touch, but hoped he wouldn't be bothered to keep her to it. Much to her relief he'd not mentioned her mother again; Gemma reckoned he'd have worked out that any threats he might make to her wouldn't match what she had on him, and she was thankful she hadn't actually had to spell it out. Thinking about it, she was still rather surprised he'd kept quiet about the poisoning and particularly about her role in it all. She hadn't let herself dwell on the momentary flicker of doubt, the brief thought that he might have something up his sleeve; nonetheless it was a little odd he hadn't gone on and on about how hard done to he felt.

Finding an apartment had turned out to have been easier than she thought. Rebecca and Victoria had been a great help and eventually she'd gone for a smart two-bedroom apartment in Holland Park Gardens, just across Holland Park Avenue from their place; and with the owner wanting a quick sale and her being a cash buyer there'd been no problems. In the end Gemma had got it for just over £75,000, a good few thousand less than she was budgeting for; the exchange of contracts was due soon and it seemed she could be in well in time for Christmas. Last weekend had convinced Gemma that she was doing the right thing. She had gone up on the Friday and stayed at Victoria and Rebecca's. It had been nice that they were so keen on having her around and on the Saturday afternoon Rebecca had helped her pick up some odds and ends for her new place from the more upmarket shops around Ladbroke Grove. After that, they'd taken a cab up to Oxford Street and she'd ordered some new furniture from the House of Fraser store; even though most of the stuff in Petworth was originally hers she didn't think it a good idea to wind Mark up too much by leaving him with nothing to sit or sleep on. Anyway she fancied a complete change and in the end had chosen a couple of brown leather, Chesterfield-style two-seater sofas and a currently fashionable platform bed which gave her more space in what was quite a small main bedroom.

The weekend hadn't just been about sorting out the internal décor of her new place. Saturday night had been her first proper date since homing in on Mark shortly after his release from HMP Ford, getting on for two years ago. Simon had picked her up and driven them up to the Hammersmith Odeon; AC/DC had been doing their *For Those About to Rock* tour for almost a year and this was the last of their four nights there. Gemma was hardly a fan of heavy metal but a free gig and backstage passes sounded good. Last time she'd seen Simon, at Annabel's, he'd looked the stereotypical young City trader, or yuppie to give them their recently acquired acronym, a slick, narrow-lapelled Armani suit and matching tie. It was strange to see his alter ego, but also oddly comforting. His black T-shirt adorned with some weird kind of mythical creature, tight blue jeans and black baseball boots hardly matched the Porsche Carrera but the incongruity worked for her. The main thing was that she'd had a great night. The band put on an undeniably brilliant show – they might have been Australian and very loud but they were bloody good. After that they'd had a few drinks, either with members of the band or part of the massive road team that accompanied them – Gemma had never been good with faces – and she and Simon had got on brilliantly too.

They'd held on to each other for most of the night and she'd enjoyed kissing him for the first time. Of course, he'd wanted to take her back to his flat in Camden and no doubt try to impress her enough to sleep with him, but she'd decided to leave that till she'd moved up to London herself. It wasn't that she was prudish, and she knew she'd enjoy it with him, but there was still a kind of loyalty to Mark and she knew it would somehow feel better once they'd actually moved apart. It was also, though, the sense the she was in control that felt good. Anyway, she had made sure Simon knew she fancied him and that he wouldn't have to wait too long. It was nice that he'd been quite gentlemanly about it all. In the end she'd let him drive her back to the flat in Holland Park; he hadn't had as much to drink as her and they'd taken enough coke to keep awake so she didn't feel overly guilty. Rebecca and Victoria were asleep, so she made him a coffee and gave him a 'next time I promise' kiss. She liked the fact that he had tried to persuade her to let him stay. To be fair by then she had been pretty tempted herself; in fact she would have been rather pissed off if he hadn't at least tried, but was pleased she'd stuck to her plan. She had always been good at that. Thinking back, Gemma felt a definite glow of satisfaction. It seemed a future was unfolding itself almost unilaterally; and it felt quite good.

***

Gemma knew that she had to try and keep her excitement at moving away from looking too obvious. She had spent the afternoon in the cottage sorting out what she was going to take to London and what was going to be left there. Mark had gone off on some kind of mission and she'd promised to make them something to eat later. Now that things were falling into place for her Gemma just wanted it to be as painless as possible with Mark.

She'd started frying the onions and mince and decided on spaghetti Bolognese; shepherd's pie had crossed her mind but the inevitable association with poisoning and murders probably meant they would never be able to face that dish again.

It was a little before six when Mark's Escort pulled up at the side of the house, accompanied by the usual scrunching of tyres and yanking of the hand brake. She saw him grab some sort of folder from the back seat; he had an oddly determined, slightly manic, look about him. He came in, opened a can of lager from the fridge and called Gemma over in an oddly presumptive manner.

'Look Gemma, I know you're going to move out and I know I've got to move on; and I do know you've been fair enough with the house and things but I don't want it to just end with you moving out, I'd like us to do something together first. And that's what I've been trying to sort out today.'

Gemma checked the meat, added a sprinkle of mixed herbs, put a pan of water on the hob for the pasta and came over.

'Well, what do you mean?'

'I'd like to go away for a few days before you leave, just us two, as a proper goodbye. Anyway, I've been into a couple of travel agents, in Farnham actually, and there's a cruise around the East Mediterranean leaving Southampton next week. It's only for a week and the late deal is really good. It calls in at Malta or Naples I think and then Dubrovnik in Yugoslavia. What do you reckon?'

It hadn't been what she expected and Gemma was thrown a little off guard.

'I don't know, I've got lots to do here and don't you think it might just make things more difficult between us?'

Apparently not; Mark was clearly full of it.

'Well, I've read up on it and it'll be great and we can easily afford it. Look, why not at least celebrate what we've done before we finally split up? It will be fun, I promise, and I've not gone anywhere since I've been out of prison.'

Even though Gemma wasn't convinced that he had really come to terms with things she had to admit it made a change to see him being reasonably positive.

'It's a bit of a surprise you know, Mark, but look, give me a little time to have a think.'

She was playing for time really, but then there was also a sort of odd attraction to the idea. Mark and her had got on, they'd done what she wanted, maybe a final goodbye trip wouldn't be such a bad idea. It could be a toast to what they'd done; and it might make Mark easier to manage once she'd left. She was well aware that he probably thought it would be a way for him to persuade her to change her mind but she knew that would never happen; even though they'd had some pretty decent times together it had always had the veneer of pragmatism for her. He probably thought a week's cruise with him would get her to realise, or from his point of view to remind her, how wonderful he was. It was quite comforting to see that he hadn't lost his almost unshakeable arrogance. She left it for now but had already decided 'Why not?'

'Look, let's have the spaghetti and I'll think about it. But bloody hell, Mark, if we do this, it's not about us staying together, it's a goodbye trip – you've got to understand that.'

It seemed that that was enough for Mark, for now at least.

'Yes absolutely. It's just I really think we deserve it, after all we've done.'

PART FOUR: LATE AUTUMN 1982

Tuesday 2 November 1982

Mark was lying on his bed with his first cup of tea of the day. They had pulled out of Southampton early on Saturday morning, and last night had done the short trip around the shoe of Italy, from the Bay of Naples to Dubrovnik. As they approached the port the Yugoslavian coastline seemed no more than a few yards from their cabin window. The new and half-finished apartments and hotels stretching out beyond and to the south of the old walled city itself evidenced Dubrovnik's growing reputation as a tourist attraction. Mark felt that at last he had some control again, that he had some sort of plan and that things were going according to it. Gemma had gone up to the sun deck earlier; even though it was late autumn, it was still warm enough to justify that name and the early morning views over the Adriatic looked pretty spectacular even from his cabin window, or porthole to use the appropriate nautical equivalent.

Once Gemma had agreed to come on this farewell trip, and to use some of the money they had got from their legacy for it, Mark had swung into action. Fair enough, it was her family's money rather than 'theirs', but it had certainly helped that they had opened a joint bank account when they had bought the house in Petworth together. At the time, Mark had never seen things coming to this; he really had believed that things would be different with Gemma. However, having the joint account had certainly turned out to be a stroke of luck. As well as paying for the cruise he had managed to withdraw most of the money they'd got from selling the various antiques and paintings that Gemma's family, really her granddad and dad, had accrued. He had been surprised that there was getting on for £55,000 there; he reckoned Gemma must have put some of the money she'd got after her father had died in that account as well. It was a shame she hadn't put the money from the sale of the house in Farnham there but there was still plenty. Anyway, apart from the hundred pounds or so he'd left in it to avoid the hassle of actually closing the account, it was now all hidden away in the lining of his suitcase. Fortunately it had been quite a rush to get everything sorted in time for the trip and Gemma had left him to it and he was pretty sure she hadn't been into town to check how much he'd taken from the account. In fact, she had spent most of the last week or so on the phone to estate agents or solicitors and had been up to London again, apparently to sign some documents to do with the flat she was buying. At least it had kept her busy and left him to get on with his back-up plan. Although a part of him still hoped that things might work out with Gemma, that spending some quality time with him would help her see sense and decide to stay with him, being realistic he had to assume that wouldn't happen and that he needed to make sure he looked after his own interests.

In any case, it wasn't as if he was doing anything unfair; the thing was, he deserved it. As well as having to inveigle his way into her mother's affections and then oversee her premature death, he was the one who had done all the legwork in getting a good price for the bits and pieces left in the Farnham house. As well as that and whatever she might have promised him, legally Gemma would still have the money from their house in Petworth when she sold it, plus her shares and the flat in London she was in the process of buying, presumably with the money from her mother's house. More to the point, did she really think that he would just accept her handout and leave it at that, take a pay-off as some kind of hired assassin and then walk off into the sunset after all they, but mainly he, had done? At least now he would have enough to start again; and if it did come to it, and that was undoubtedly the most likely scenario, he would have to make some kind of new life for himself. At least he had no real ties back in England either, because going back almost certainly wouldn't be an option.

Mark had realised, within a couple of days after Gemma had told him that as far as she was concerned they had no future together, that she was serious. Of course, he'd felt angry and let down but that hadn't got in the way of him starting to make his own plans. Fair enough, if by chance they did end up staying together he could cover his tracks, but if she thought this cruise was just a desperate attempt to persuade her to stay with him and that he would have been too upset to consider any alternatives, she didn't know him as well as she reckoned. He'd been through absolute chaos and more with Justine, it wasn't going to happen a second time. He may have been misled before, he certainly had taken his eye off the ball with her but that was then. Musing over things since the early hours and as the SS Uganda rounded the south-eastern tip of Italy he had realised that even though he had been putting his doubts about Gemma to the back of his mind over the last few months, they had clearly been there and were clearly merited as well. Mark was well aware that he had a tendency to put his head in the sand, but over the last few weeks he had been keeping an eye on Gemma and had formed the distinct impression that, in spite of her apparent openness and plausibility, something had been going on. That must have been why he had checked up on her accounts of her trips to London; and even though it went against the grain to spy and was hardly the epitome of the coolness and laid-back approach he liked to accord to himself, he was glad he had. Her excuse for staying an extra night on a couple of occasions had started him off: after all, you could get up to London in an hour from theirs. He had made a point of helping to bring her bags in after her last trip to London and managed to have a quick rummage through when she wasn't hovering over them. The laced negligee and matching knickers hardly seemed the thing for a night or two staying at her friends' flat and a somewhat crumpled ticket from an AC/DC gig didn't strike him as the sort of thing her snobby girlfriends would be likely to be into.

While he had been making arrangements for the cruise, Mark had felt himself getting to the point of not giving a damn about the consequences; and it was something of a consolation that whatever came from it all it couldn't be any worse than what he'd been through before. It really had got to the stage where he needed to get something akin to revenge, or at the very least a fair deal; and if as it seemed Gemma had abandoned him, that was where he'd get it. The idea of dealing with Gemma in any way other than financially hadn't crossed his mind when he had initially suggested the cruise. However the frustration and annoyance he'd felt when she had just assumed that that was it between them had been smouldering away and developing into feelings closer to anger and betrayal. In particular, the sense of having been used and having not been aware of it had been building as he had started to make steps to ensure he wasn't left high and dry. It had given him some focus as well as justification. If she thought that she could play him for a fool then she needed to be taught a lesson. And what was wrong with revenge? Retribution had always seemed to him to be the most sensible justification for any form of punishment. However, the main thing was to get what he deserved and the fifty thousand-plus would fit the bill there.

Of course, he was well aware that should anything happen to Gemma everything would point to him, but no matter what suspicions may and would arise, if it came to it he would leave absolutely no trace this time around. And there'd be no confession either; her mates would be sure to assume it was him but they'd have no evidence. This time there wouldn't be a need for any convoluted or slow-burning poisoning, apart from anything else Gemma would be on the look-out for that.

It would have to be an accident, either in one of the ports they visited or, even if a bit dramatic, over the side at night, maybe a domestic row that got out of hand. He reckoned one of their stop-overs would be the best bet and from the little bit of reading around he'd had time to do, Dubrovnik seemed a possibility.

Mulling it over Mark couldn't really explain where it had all that come from. He pulled on his shirt and jeans in a state close to semi-shock. Ripping off Gemma or more accurately taking his deserved share was one thing, but he had just let his mind wander way beyond that. Sure, it had been at the back of his mind as a possible last resort, but now, thinking it through, he realised it would be a lot easier without having Gemma to deal with in future; and she was hardly likely to let him just walk off with her money. He could feel a surge of adrenalin: maybe that was the solution and he merely hadn't liked to accept it before the trip. Feeling that he was in charge of his fate, Mark finished dressing and went up to the deck to find Gemma. For the time being it was probably best to see how the next day or two played out.

The cruise had been a bit of a brainwave; they'd be away from England and depending on how it all panned out he could just leave and go to ground in Italy, Yugoslavia, Greece or wherever felt right. Cruising was beginning to become a popular holiday option and living near to Southampton had helped. Mark had wanted them to be as anonymous as possible and had aimed to get them on as large a ship as he could. Initially he had tried to book with P&O on the SS Canberra. However even though it had been re-fitted since being requisitioned as some sort of troop carrier during the Falklands War earlier that year, and had returned to its civilian role a few weeks back in September, it wasn't offering any suitable Mediterranean trips that winter. The SS Uganda was a good deal smaller but there were places available and he felt more comfortable with the Med than going any further afield. In fact, it was all beginning to work out better than he had planned or even feared. The trip had cost them – and so, effectively, him, given that he had just about emptied their account – less than he'd expected and it looked as if it had been a stroke of luck that one of the options had ended with the two nights in Dubrovnik. As it was a one-way cruise with passengers flying back to various airports in Britain from the different stop-over points, there'd be no real reason for Gemma or him to be missed should they leave before the end of the itinerary. Presumably it would be assumed they'd missed their flights or just decided to continue their holiday.

Today the plan was to go into the old town and do some sight-seeing and exploring; then after a final night on board and the usual heavy breakfast, and assuming he hadn't got it wrong and Gemma and him were really over, he'd do what was needed with her and melt into a new life, maybe making his way across to the Greek islands, perhaps Crete for a while at least. Mark had stayed there one summer a few years ago when a student and enjoyed the easy-going atmosphere. He had managed to get some work in a bar with no questions being asked.

Mark had had no real plan at the beginning of the trip, apart from a vague idea of some kind of accident-cum-drowning if things didn't work out. However after Gemma had gone back to their cabin once they had eaten last night, he'd spent the rest of the evening drinking with Derek and Jude, an oldish couple of regular cruisers who'd told him about the little island of Lokrum that snuggled in the bay a few hundred metres from Dubrovnik itself. They had seemed pleased to have someone younger to impress and Derek, in particular, had revelled in being allowed to show off his knowledge of the area, and of life in general. Apparently Lokrum had been the home to Benedictine monks for centuries up to the early 1800s but, apart from being used as a holiday home by Archduke Maximilian of Austria for a few years in the mid-nineteenth century, it had been uninhabited ever since. However it was open to visitors in the day time with regular ferries to and fro from the port of Dubrovnik. Aside from the remains of the monastery, a few paths and a small café, it was largely wooded, although there was a deep salt water lake there, apparently ideal for swimming. Derek and Jude had visited on each of their previous trips to Dubrovnik and, between G & Ts and pints, had explained how it was the perfect place to get away from everyone and everything, and particularly so in late autumn. Their implication, albeit in their slightly inebriated state by the end of the evening, was that a young couple like himself and Gemma could get back to nature and 'do their thing', as it was rather inelegantly put. In fact, they had mentioned there was some sort of nudist beach there too, although November probably wasn't the time to explore that. For Mark, though, it had sowed the seeds of a plan. When he had returned to their cabin for

164

the night, Gemma had been awake still and he'd suggested they visited Lokrum on one of the two final days of the trip.

As the Uganda dropped anchor between Dubrovnik and the island itself he could see what Derek and Jude had meant. The outline of the island, dark green, almost black, against the horizon and early morning light, with the waves from the liner lapping gently along a deserted shoreline, evidenced no signs of habitation.

***

Gemma put down her copy of Robert Ludlum's latest story of espionage and skulduggery, *The Parsifal Mosaic*, stretched lazily out of the deck chair, pulled her jacket around her shoulders and wandered down to their cabin to see if Mark was going to bother with breakfast before the first ferry of the day to the old city. She liked a good thriller but this one on the Cold War hadn't gripped her in the same way as *The Bourne Identity* or some of his other previous books, and especially *The Scarlatti Inheritance*, had. This one was a little far-fetched and samey; still, it was alright as holiday reading and nice that bits were set around the Mediterranean. It had been a pleasant start to the final day of the cruise and all in all and in spite of her misgivings she had enjoyed the trip so far. The weather had been unusually mild for early November and the brief stopovers in Malta and Naples had been fascinating, if a little rushed. Mark hadn't been too much of a strain either. Even though he'd agreed not to expect anything, they had decided to share a cabin and she'd actually let him sleep with her on the second night, partly to keep him quiet but mainly because sleeping on board had turned her on – and why not? After all, if he couldn't cope with it that was his look out. The thing was that Mark had been really easy-going, in fact in a quite out of character manner, and they had got on remarkably well for what was definitely for her a last goodbye. She had noticed that he'd seemed somewhat distracted too, as if he had something on his mind, but she really couldn't be bothered to worry or even think about him or what was going on in his head. They had made an arrangement to have this final holiday and that was it as far as Gemma was concerned.

She made her way down to the cabins, checking that breakfast was being served in the dining area. Before she had reached the cabin deck she bumped into Mark who was on his way to find her. He was dressed and looked ready to go.

'Come on Mark, let's grab a quick bite and get the ferry into the town, it looks absolutely gorgeous and it's going to be a nice day by all accounts.'

She gathered her things for the day and reminded herself that she needed to get to a post office or somewhere she could phone her solicitors and bank to check that the details on the sale of her flat in London were being tidied up and it was going ahead as planned.

After a quick breakfast, they joined quite a number of their fellow passengers to clamber down to the ship's tender for the short trip across to the harbour, which apparently wasn't deep enough to take the larger ships themselves. It wasn't a problem for Gemma or Mark but the climb down the side of the Uganda was clearly something of an ordeal for one or two who, along with a good proportion of the cruisers, looked well into their retirement years. It was certainly the case that cruising was generally seen as the ideal holiday for older folk. In spite of being just about the youngest passengers, that hadn't bothered Gemma or Mark either. In fact the lack of the stereotypical two-plus-two families, and of children in general, was quite refreshing; indeed, the couples on their trip didn't hold back on eating or drinking and were generally pretty decent company. They weren't overly bothered about the state of their lungs or the shape of their bodies and were happy to sit around talking and drinking day or night. Both of them, but perhaps particularly Mark, had enjoyed a few late-night sessions with whoever was around and willing.

It was a little after ten when they disembarked at the old harbour, with a good four or five hours to look around before the return trip. Gemma suggested they split up and explore on their own.

'I'm going to do some clothes shopping which isn't your thing, I know, so why don't you look around yourself? I may do the city walls too, so let's just meet at the harbour around three for the ferry back. I haven't forgotten you mentioned going over to that island but we could do that tomorrow after they throw us off the boat. We've got hours before the flight home and anyway we could always re-arrange that if we had to.'

Mark could hardly believe it and was happy to agree. It was as if Gemma had read his mind; surely she couldn't have guessed what had been going on in his head for the last few day. He put the thought aside.

'Yes, good idea. I wouldn't mind looking round the old cathedral and there's a couple of museums that Derek and his wife were telling me about last night.'

That was true, anyway. Ever since he had been taken to virtually every cathedral in Britain as part of their family holidays when he was a boy, Mark had always retained a real and genuine fascination with those buildings. The proportions, the windows, the pillars and ceilings had an inspirational quality he was unavoidably and deeply touched by. It never ceased to amaze him that they had been built before the tools and machinery available and taken for granted nowadays. He'd read about the baroque style of the cathedral in Dubrovnik in an old *Baedeker* guide the travel agent had lent him; it had been renovated over the last few years and Mark was keen to have a look. His more recent and up-to-date *Lonely Planet* guide book had mentioned that during the renovation another even older cathedral dating back to the seventh century had been discovered under the foundations of what had until then been thought to be the original cathedral, which was itself badly damaged by an earthquake in the seventeenth century. He loved maps and travel guides and couldn't understand why people visited places without finding out as much as possible about them.

***

As Gemma wandered off through the gate leading from the harbour into town, Mark strolled around the jetty and past a few fishermen pottering about in a desultory fashion, mending nets and baskets and doing whatever they did when they had managed to get rid of their catches. He took a few photos and walked up to the town himself. It was certainly impressive. The marble effect of the main streets sparkled in the autumnal sun; it really did look like marble although he recalled that the *Baedeker* book had said something about hard limestone. The various shops and cafés on the Placa, the main street running up through the middle of the town, were already geared up for their day's activity. Mark strolled up to the Franciscan church and monastery, just before the main entrance gate of the city walls, at the top of the Placa. He sat down by the stone fountain opposite; the monastery didn't appear to be open, and after a quick glance at the useful street map in his *Lonely Planet* guide he decided to make his way through the smaller side streets back to the cathedral and then perhaps try to find somewhere for a sandwich and drink.

The maze of streets and alleys had led him almost back to the port again when he came across the cathedral. Appearing quite suddenly, almost by surprise, it was imposing without being overpowering. The surrounding square seemed a little dowdy and certainly low-key, but the four columns on the front façade were grand enough. Mark entered the nave which was surprisingly bright and spacious: it gave the impression of being too large for the outside of the building. There was some pretty stunning glass and artwork too, including a 16th century work by Titian that must have survived the earthquake. He wasn't sure about the policy on taking photographs but there weren't many visitors inside and only a couple of what he assumed must be local worshippers so he managed to sneak in a good few pictures. Being bothered to take photos struck him as a little strange; he wondered who he'd ever have to show them to. After all, it wouldn't be Gemma and he wasn't intending to go back to England for a good while either. Still, there would no doubt be someone, he was sure of that.

It was past midday when Mark emerged into the sunlight and he was ready to find somewhere to sit down and eat. Although the *Baedeker* wasn't much help with places to eat and drink, his *Lonely Planet* book on travelling in Europe had mentioned a small café-cum-bar in Dubrovnik, situated on one of the steep streets just off the Placa and running up to the residential areas of the town, apparently either managed or owned by an English couple. Mark headed back into the centre of the old town to look in to it.

Sure enough, by the time he got to the third or fourth side street he spotted a small Union Jack hovering across the narrow passageway, more than street, that separated the buildings on one side from those on other. There were a couple of tables outside but there was little chance of the winter sun reaching them, let alone the summer one, Mark thought. He went in and sat at a table near the window and let his eyes adjust to the lack of light. Apart from him there were only a couple of what looked to be local builders eating some kind of pasties with their coffees. There was a pile of magazine and papers on a bench by the door and he picked up a copy of the *Sunday Times* magazine from a couple of weeks back. That was an encouraging sign, he reckoned. Earlier in the day, he had exchanged just a few pounds into what seemed to be a massive amount of dinars and he ordered a coffee from a waitress who clearly wasn't English while deciding which sandwich to go for. As she brought it over he gave a sudden start, behind her and emerging from what he assumed must be the back kitchen was someone who looked strangely familiar. He couldn't place when or where but Mark was certain he knew him; surely not from his time in prison. After a second take it came to him: it wasn't from prison, it was from his university days, and when as a student rather than lecturer. He was sure it was Howard, the quiet lad who'd been in his year at Kent and in a couple of his Sociology classes. He remembered they'd chatted on occasion, mainly about the course and essays, and he had seemed a decent enough type, if a little uncool by Mark's standards at the time, however embarrassingly dated those seemed now. Mark stood up and called over to him.

'My God Howard, is that you? It's Mark, we were at uni together.'

Howard put the grubby pair of oven gloves he was carrying on the counter, took off his glasses and came across to Mark's table, staring at him.

'Yes so it is, wow, what are you doing here?'

He looked more shocked than Mark.

'I don't believe it, I read all about you, you were all over the news.'

Mark had never really taken the time to consider how people he had known just in passing before the murders and his imprisonment would have reacted and he could see he would have to explain things to Howard.

'Yes it must have been a shock to people, but look, Howard, I was stupid and did some mad things; but don't worry, I'm not some sort of out of control maniac killer. And I've come over here to start again and rebuild things.'

He thought it probably best not to tell Howard that he was in Dubrovnik as part of a plan for another possible but certainly final murder.

'It must be more than ten years since I last saw you, Howard.'

Howard pulled a chair over and sat down. He was tall and thin, skinny really, and quite tanned; even in a somewhat greasy T-shirt and jeans Mark reckoned he looked better than he had done as a student in the late 'sixties. Even in his work clothes, he exuded a confidence and sense of control that certainly hadn't been apparent back then.

'No I'm not one to judge, but it's amazing to see you here. I'll get a bottle of our local wine and you can tell me what happened. I mean, what are you doing here?'

'Yes, it's weird seeing you again, you look like you're sort of at home here, though. Actually I'm on the cruise liner that arrived this morning, I've got to get back to the harbour around three but it'd be great to catch up.'

Howard brought a bottle of red over and asked Lana, the waitress, to bring some bread and cheese and to deal with another couple of locals who'd just come in to the bar. He was obviously intrigued to find out just what had happened. And judging from the way he talked to Lana he was obviously more than just a part-time waiter.

'You know we all thought you were so hip, I was a little in awe of you at uni; you probably don't remember but I got some pot off you and Tom a couple of times. What happened to Tom? I mean I heard you'd got a job at Sussex University and then, years later, a mate of mine called me and said he'd heard you were on trial for murder. It was massive news.'

The atmosphere in the café bar was pleasant and Mark felt pretty comfy and quite happy to get things off his chest. He had lost touch with so many old friends and contacts and it felt good to have someone from back then to talk to. He launched into it.

'Well it's a long story but actually Tom was one of the reasons I did what I did and in the end the bastard took off with my girlfriend. You know he was really well off, well his parents were; he just flashed his money in front of her and turned her head. I know I was married but it wasn't really working and my in-laws were rolling in it. I needed to sort things for me and Justine, she was my girlfriend and Tom knew I was planning on leaving my wife and being with her. Anyway, as you no doubt heard, I got rid of them to get my hands on some real money. I was only trying to get a future for me and Justine sorted until he intervened; in any case it's water under the bridge now. I served my time as they say, over six years and the thing is that there is no future back there for me now. Actually I've got a decent stash of money, enough to invest in something and start a new life somewhere. But look what about you? Tell me what you're doing here.'

Howard poured them both another glass.

'Okay, but I'm not letting you go without finding out all about things. You murdered them – poisoned, I seem to remember. Bloody hell, Mark, I did read about it once I'd heard it was you.'

'Fair enough, if we get a chance I'll tell you all about it, but how come you're here?'

Howard took a packet of Malboros out of his shirt pocket and offered Mark one.

'Well, I came over soon after finishing at Kent, just for the summer initially but I met this Croatian girl, Branka, and came back the following year and basically stayed here. She had a bit of family money and we decided to open this place. Her family were great; they could see tourism beginning to take off in the area and helped out. I've done a lot of the legwork to get it started and they've helped with the legal and official stuff, and it's going okay. In fact, we're thinking of expanding things. We're married now but she's not around today, gone to see her sister in Split for a day or two.'

As he listened, Mark could sense the beginnings of an opportunity opening up, particularly when Howard mentioned that they needed a bigger place to cope with the demand. Even though President Tito had died a couple of years previously and there was a good deal of financial instability in the country, his lengthy period in power had helped create a more modern Yugoslavia and a degree of freedom from the Soviet domination of Eastern Europe. That had opened the country, and especially Dubrovnik itself, up to western tourists, as evidenced by the flurry of hotel building on the hill up from the old town, along with its developing role as a cruise stopover.

'Look Howard, this could be just what I'm looking for you know – it's what they call serendipity, perhaps. Like I said, I haven't got much to go back for and I've got some money, quite a bit, and plenty of energy as well. Look why don't we talk some more, maybe tomorrow?'

Mark sensed that Howard looked less than enthusiastic but put it down to not having had time to think things through. He pushed on.

'I know it's a bit sudden and no pressure, Howard. Thing is I'm going over to Lokrum tomorrow morning and was due to fly back in the evening but over the last few days I've decided to stay over in Europe for a while at least. Why don't I come round later tomorrow? Even if nothing comes of things it will still be good to catch up, and you can give me some advice, no doubt. I've got to dash now, said I'd meet someone for the taxi-ferry back.'

Howard agreed; when he thought about it, what harm could it do? And anyway it would be interesting to catch up. After all, Mark's crimes had been a major talking point on the odd occasions that he had met up with any of his old university mates. Also, although quite happy with his new life, Howard still missed England and English people and even though he hadn't known Mark particularly well before there was no reason they couldn't get on now.

'Yes, why not? And like I said, you must tell me about what really happened.'

'Great, that's settled then. I've got to dash now, as I said I've got to meet someone for the taxi-ferry back to the ship.'

Mark thought it best not to mention Gemma by name and anyway Howard had been more interested in his past than his current status. He thanked the still slightly perplexed Howard for the drink and food and headed back to the harbour. He felt good: maybe that was the break he needed and it might change everything. After all, there'd be no need to get rid of Gemma, he would just tell her that she'd won and that he'd leave her alone to get on with her life; and the money he'd taken was fair enough given all he'd helped her with. In fact, after the initial shock when she first got to realise what he'd done, she'd cope with things. There would be no need to tell her before she flew back. Of course she might not be too happy he'd taken it behind her back, but she'd get over it; she still had more than enough, plenty of shares in Cunard's, and she could sell their house and keep that for herself. In fact, she was bloody lucky; his stake in the Petworth house would have given him close to the amount he had taken anyway. Really, if it was looked at rationally he'd be doing everyone a favour.

Mark passed the elegant sixteenth-century Sponza Palace and went through the gates to what was already becoming known as the 'old' port. Yes, why would he want to stay with Gemma even if by some chance she had changed her mind again? He'd be fine and find someone who wouldn't let him down this time. And why risk another murder, however well-planned and hidden it might be? As far as he was concerned she could sod off, and there was no need to tell her just yet about his meeting with Howard and his ideas for the future. He would merely say goodbye and head off to meet Howard when she went to the airport tomorrow night.

***

There was a winding down of the day's activities on the harbour side as Mark headed to the jetty for the taxi-boat back to the Uganda. He could see Gemma already standing by the rails of the gangway. Sure enough she was a bloody good looking girl but he'd had enough of self-centred prima donnas who thought they could outsmart him. He smiled as he reached her.

'Hi, how's things? What do you reckon of Dubrovnik, then?'

Gemma had decided to leave telling Mark what she had been up to or what she had managed to discover, for the time being anyway. She felt she'd be better off just playing it straight for now, until she sensed that the time was right to confront him.

'Well it's beautiful, the architecture and the views too; it'll be interesting to visit Lokrum tomorrow, everyone I've spoken to says it's worth exploring and it's quiet at this time of year too.'

Even though his intentions had changed and it wasn't necessary now, Mark didn't see any reason not to go there as planned, even if they would both be going their separate ways afterwards.

***

Gemma's day hadn't turned out as she'd expected. She had wanted to check out if there were any clothes that might give her something a little different from the high street fashions back in England and maybe to pick up a few souvenirs or even early Christmas presents. She was also a little concerned that she hadn't managed to speak to her solicitors about the purchase of the flat in London, which should be close to going through by now – if it was going to be completed soon after she got back, she figured that it should at least be at the contract signing stage by now. She had tried to call a couple of times but with no luck: the connections from the ship weren't very reliable. It wasn't that she was particularly bothered, it just would be nice to know all was well before she returned home. The post office in Dubrovnik seemed the obvious place to start, and if nothing else she could check the bank balance which would give her an idea of whether everything was in place.

The gift shops on the Placa were gearing up for the day's business, commandeering their sections of the pavement and competing with the tables and umbrellas of the various coffee bars and cafés. Even though it was early November, the bright sun reflecting off the marble effect pavement gave the whole scene, from the clock tower and Sponza Palace to the Franciscan monastery and entrance to the old city through the Gothic arches of the Pile Gate at the top of the street, a touristy feel.

Gemma popped into one of the stores and was set on by a deeply weather-worn, elderly woman who presumably owned or managed the place and who was keen to extol in surprisingly understandable English the virtues of the range of knick-knacks available. There were few tourists around and Gemma felt a little sorry for her. Even though she would probably be back before it arrived, Gemma chose a postcard to send to Victoria and Rebecca, along with a couple of key rings and a mug embossed with scenes of the walled city. She walked further up the main thoroughfare and the distinctive yellow Posta sign soon came into view. The post office was set amongst the tradesmen's workshops and small shops just off Ulica od Puca to the left of the Placa itself. Thankfully it was quiet and she sorted enough change to phone the solicitors and bank if needed. As she had found on the previous times she'd tried, the solicitors' phone sounded as if it was ringing but there was no answer. It took a couple of tries before there was an answer from the Barclays branch in Littlehampton, where she had kept their account even after Mark had been added to it when they bought the house in Petworth and moved away from the town. After she had convinced the cashier there that she was a genuine customer – thank goodness she remembered her mother's maiden name – she was given the balance. It was just under £100. It took a moment to register; that couldn't be right. Too confused to respond, Gemma said thanks and put the phone down in a state of shock that must have been felt a thousand miles away in Sussex. She knew that Mark was going to pay for the holiday from it but there was all the money they'd got from the sale of the paintings, furniture and everything else from her family's estate. There should have been thousands in there.

Gemma sat down on one of the metal-framed canvas chairs, conveniently placed around the large post office hall; it crossed her mind that they were perhaps there for disturbed customers to gather their thoughts. After a couple of minutes she got some more dinara coins from the front desk and phoned the bank again. She was answered by the same man and explained that she couldn't understand the figure he had just given her and asked him to check again. Sure enough all but one hundred pounds had been withdrawn from her current account on the day before the holiday by one of the account holders. It made some kind of sense now, and of course it wasn't just her account.

A surge of panic hit her: what if the flat sale had somehow gone ahead without her knowing? Although it didn't make much sense, maybe there had been some sort of transfer of funds ready for her buying the flat. However, surely that couldn't be the case: she was certain she had kept the Farnham money in a separate account. She tried the solicitor's again and eventually they picked up. One of the junior clerks reassured her.

'No, there's been no sign of the completion being sorted on the apartment in Holland Park. And anyway you would have to sign a few more papers before that could happen. Is anything the matter?'

Gemma needed to compose herself; there was no point in letting anything out till she'd got to the bottom of things.

'No, just checking how things were, thanks for your help.'

She left the post office; she needed to sit down and needed to work things out. She went to the nearest café and ordered a black coffee.

So that was his plan, the bastard. All that talk about a final holiday, a nice way to part and so on, but what the hell was he up to? Gemma realised she hadn't checked their joint account for weeks, there'd been no need to. None of the new cash machines had appeared in Petworth yet and she hadn't been down to Littlehampton in the last couple of weeks, and anyway she'd known it was in a pretty healthy state so there'd been no need to worry. She did a quick mental tally: with some money she'd put in plus the various things they'd sold from her family's house she assumed there must have been around £50,000, if not more, there; anyway, she could find that out from the bank later. The question was, what was she going to do about it? If he thought he'd get away with it he was even more deluded than she had imagined.

Her coffee was strong and she went to the counter to get a pastry; she needed to keep her sugar intake up. Okay, she was due to meet Mark at around three o'clock for the trip back to the Uganda and then next morning they'd agreed to go to Lokrum before the flight back to Gatwick. Of course, it must have been him who'd taken the money, but surely he wouldn't have done that and then just flown back home with her as if nothing had happened. He must have something else up his sleeve. She realised the most likely explanation was that he was probably planning to disappear with it.

Gemma got up and paid for her coffee and pastry. There were a few hours to kill so she figured she may as well have a look around the city and gather her thoughts together. The advantage was that Mark would have no idea that she knew and it would be best to keep it that way while she decided what to do. He had seemed genuine enough about wanting to visit Lokrum tomorrow so it must be after that that he planned to go. It was a lovely autumnal day so she decided to get on to the city walls and find somewhere to sit and work things through in her head. On the way up to the Pile Gate, she stopped and bought a packet of cigarettes and a lighter, something she hadn't done for years, but it somehow seemed appropriate now.

There'd be no point in confronting him straight away, that was for sure; and it would be easy enough to let him think he was in control. She'd play up to him, maybe even flirt a little on their final evening on board; pander to his basic arrogance. And she'd sort something out, there was no way he would get away with it – that money wouldn't be going anywhere with him. Gemma was annoyed with herself for not having seen anything like this coming, she had let herself get carried away with planning the move to London and maybe to Simon too.

Gemma was kind of surprised that she'd actually quite enjoyed the rest of the day by herself. She felt one step ahead and surprisingly composed; and she would make sure she got her money back. After grabbing a sandwich and can of coke it was getting time to head back to the harbour and she wanted to get there before Mark, for no particular reason but perhaps just to feel more in control.

Even though the tourist trade had virtually ended for the winter, the harbour itself remained surprisingly busy: baskets of fish were still being unloaded from a variety of sized crafts, most of which had clearly seen a good few years' service. Gemma wandered across to the railings overlooking the steps down to the usual mooring position for the cruise ship tenders. She lit her second cigarette of the day and even though it tasted as bad as the first she enjoyed seeing the smoke drift over the harbour walls. Before she had finished she noticed Mark heading through the gated entrance from the old city. She stubbed the cigarette out and flicked the dog end into the water; she didn't want him to sense anything was amiss. He looked pleased with himself, the big-headed bastard, and Gemma could see it was pretty obvious he had no idea she was onto him. Well, he wouldn't till tomorrow either; she'd bide her time and confront him on their trip to Lokrum.

Annoyingly he had seen her put the cigarette out on his way across to the jetty.

'Hey, strange to see you smoking a fag.'

Gemma forced a smile.

'Well, we're on holiday and I just fancied one. Anyway, how's your day been?'

Mark decided not to mention meeting Howard; he reckoned the less Gemma knew the better.

'Yes, what a beautiful city, I've just pottered around and met some of the locals. I had a couple of glasses of some local red wine in a little bar I found.'

Mark was full of himself; his misplaced belief that he was in control and about to get away with ripping her off amused but also irritated Gemma.

'Yes, it is really nice. You know I'm looking forward to our last meal of the trip on board tonight, apparently there's going to be some kind of band, or DJ anyway, so it should be fun. Then we've got a day out to the island tomorrow before flying home.'

Gemma couldn't resist it. She wanted to check for any kind of reaction from Mark. There wasn't even a flicker of what might pass for guilt. He certainly seemed to have got over the apparent despair he had shown when she'd told him she'd had enough and wanted to move on and away.

'Glad you're looking forward to it, you look great you know, Gemma. I know we're over but I can say that, can't I?'

The Uganda's tender was just pulling in and Gemma let it pass as they scrambled down the harbour steps along with a few other of their fellow cruisers armed with the various trinkets they'd been harangued into acquiring.

***

As well as Mark and Gemma, quite a few of the passengers were also celebrating their final evening and night on board. It wasn't the end of the cruise itself, with some staying on for further stopovers at Piraeus harbour, for Athens, and then Istanbul. Nonetheless, the ship had put on a slightly wider choice of meals than usual and a disco of sorts. Between courses there'd been a somewhat grandly entitled debarkation talk, and those leaving the next day were told that they needed to sort out the extra costs they might have incurred while on board.

The initial shock of finding that Mark had emptied their bank account had subsided and spurred Gemma into action mode. She kept Mark's glass full and made sure the second bottle came pretty quickly. As was usual and really still quite quaint, passengers were expected to dress smartly for the evening meals and entertainment on board. Gemma had made sure she'd be able to get Mark where she wanted; she'd put on a low-cut party dress and curled her hair to fall tantalisingly down either side of her still slightly tanned décolletage and deep cleavage. By contrast, Mark always managed to look uncomfortable in a shirt and tie, but she wasn't going to let that get in the way. It was clear he had no suspicions that his skulduggery had been discovered and Gemma knew the best bet was to get him drunk, add a bit of flattery and flirting and keep an eye on him when they got back to their cabin; he'd be bound to check on his stash of his, or actually her, money and no doubt to try and do it surreptitiously.

The meal itself had been nicely presented – and if a roast followed by Black Forest gateau was a little unambitious it was pleasant enough. The guests had made an effort to dress up and there was certainly more of a party atmosphere than usual. Gemma could see the waiters hovering with jugs of tea or coffee.

'Come on Mark, let's leave the coffee and have a couple of shorts, I'll get us doubles.'

She ushered him over to a table near the DJ, apparently a local resident who offered his services to visiting cruise ships, and went to the bar.

'A double vodka and Coke and I'll have a plain Coke.'

It wasn't as if he was going to monitor her drinks but she didn't want him to see she wasn't getting drunk too; from now on she was going to be in control.

'You know Mark, I've quite enjoyed this holiday and thanks for sorting it all out. I feel like having a really good time tonight and enjoying ourselves like we used to. Let's down these and go for it.'

He really was quite absurdly easy to manipulate. Gemma even felt a little light-headed herself and that was after only a couple of glasses of wine with the meal; she reckoned he must be well on his way to getting drunk. Surprisingly, the DJ seemed to be more on the ball than they might have expected and in spite of a limited selection of discs hadn't veered back into the 'sixties yet. Even though Mark prided himself on having the coolest tastes in music, Gemma was amused to see his reaction to the first distinctive chords of 'C'mon Eileen'.

'Look at you rocking to Dexy's Midnight Runners! Come on, let's have a dance.'

She grabbed Mark and pushed him onto the small dance space – floor would be putting it too grandly. By the time that had merged into 'The Lion Sings Tonight' by the oddly named Tight Fit, they had been joined by a good few of the other guests.

Gemma needed to make sure his guard was completely down.

'This is great Mark, I'm getting quite out of it. I think we might have a good time in the cabin later. Let's have another drink beforehand, though.'

She could see Mark thought he was the one seducing her, silly sod. It amused her that as he got more drunk Mark's eye contact lowered to an almost permanent fixation on to her cleavage – glancing down herself it wasn't difficult to imagine what it was that men found so enticing.

'Here, you sit down, I like going to the bar.'

Gemma got him another double and another plain coke for her. As she wended her way back to their table she could see Mark was looking a bit the worse for wear. She didn't want him to completely pass out straight away, that was for sure. Of course she could try to locate the money he must have hidden somewhere but that might prove a little difficult in the cramped space of their cabin. The best bet would be to wait for him to check his things. Mark was pretty tidy by nature and certainly liked to keep a close eye on his money; if she didn't make it obvious she reckoned he'd be bound to give something away.

She brought the drinks over and gave him a quick hug.

'Let's take them up on to the deck, get some fresh air and have a cig.'

The night air was cool rather than cold and the lights of Dubrovnik sparkled across the bay, contrasting with the dark outline of the island of Lokrum from the other side of the ship, she could never remember which was port and which starboard.

Gemma put her arm through Mark's. Lighting a cigarette, she heard Boy George's distinctive voice begin the lyrics of 'Do You Really Want to Hurt Me?' How appropriate, and that bastard really had, or certainly had intended to. She'd make sure it was the other way around before they left tomorrow.

'Come on Mark, let's go back to the cabin.'

This was proving easier than she'd imagined, although the whole thing was also tainted with an unmistakeable air of depression. It should never have come to this. Mark really looked and sounded quite ridiculous when drunk; what had she seen in him and how had she managed to waste the last two years? Actually that was rather unfair, the sad thing was that there had been some good times and Mark wasn't such a bad guy to have met, but it was never going to be forever for her. In any case that was a little beside the point: this all needed to be sorted out, now wasn't the time for any detailed self-analysis or recrimination. While hardly seeing herself as fatalistic, Gemma liked to believe that things happened for a reason. She didn't regret it all, but he was the one who messed everything up; they could have just moved on without any hassle if he hadn't been such a thieving bastard.

Gemma pushed Mark onto his bed, there wasn't much room to go anywhere else anyway. Although still limited for space, at least Mark had managed to book one of the bigger cabins with twin beds. There was just about room for a chair and two built-in cupboards, which was a good deal more than some of the other cabins she'd glanced into.

'Ok Mark let's have some fun on our last night aboard.'

She took off his tie and undid his shirt. Normally that would have been the signal for him to try and take control but he looked pretty wrecked this time. Maybe she wouldn't even have to grin and bear it. She unzipped his trousers and pulled them down over his legs and ankles. She realised that the way Mark was it should be easy enough to check out his luggage without waiting for him to give things away. Pulling his socks off she moved her hand up his legs and into his somewhat passé Y-fronts. It was fairly obvious he wouldn't be up to anything for the time being at least. Gemma kissed him on the lips, pulled the blanket over his virtually inert frame and whispered that she would put his clothes in his case ready for tomorrow.

There was no response. Gemma hadn't really taken a lot of notice of the large suitcase Mark had brought with him. Only now did it strike her as excessive for the limited clothing he seemed to have with him. She gave him another kiss to check and, somewhat unnecessarily given his state, whispered for him to lie back and wait for her. Her mind was clear and it felt good to be back in control. She wasn't happy that she'd let Mark get as far as he had, and as close as he had to ripping her off; she'd taken her eye off things. Even though he was well away she had to make sure that when Mark did come round he assumed they'd just crashed out together. She needed to be quick and then get back into his bed and drape herself around him.

Fifty-plus grand would amount to a fairly decent sized package and he'd have had to take some care getting it out of the country, although to be fair it was rare to get much attention from HM Customs when leaving, and probably especially when on a cruise ship. It must be in the suitcase lining somewhere, the classic hiding place. She'd have to get to it and fill any space left with something – maybe a couple of her magazines would do. Gemma had noticed there was an empty cabin just down their corridor, it had been used by an elderly couple who'd left the cruise a couple of days before in Italy. For no particular reason apart from nosiness, she'd looked in earlier that evening when passing. She'd been surprised it was left open but then there was nothing in it and everyone else had their own cabins so there wasn't any need for security. She put her face to Mark's and murmured that she'd be joining him soon; he was well away still. Quickly she pulled the case from under his bed and across the corridor to the empty cabin, smaller than theirs with bunk beds and just about room to manoeuvre. Just as she'd expected, a tear in the side of the lining and her money neatly packed away in large envelopes. He hadn't even bothered to sew the lining back – typical of his arrogance, no doubt; he really did think he was invincible. Gemma pulled the money out, put it all into a carrier bag and stuffed her magazines back between the outside of the case and the lining.

With Mark's suitcase safely back under his bed and his planned escape route and strategy now securely hidden in her own smaller travel bag she got in next to him. She could arrange getting the money back home in due course; probably through some kind of bank transfer which she'd have to check out in Dubrovnik before flying home. That was the least of her concerns; she still had tomorrow to deal with Mark. With the adrenalin still flowing she couldn't sleep. In fact, the whole thing had made her quite horny and she tried briefly but unsuccessfully to get him to respond; maybe she'd try again in the morning – after all, she was in charge now, so why not? It would help keep him off-guard, too. He was always easier to deal with after sex.

Wednesday 3 November 1982

Gemma woke from a fitful sleep just after seven. She could just make out a wintry sun already beginning to catch the higher parts of the old city. She checked again that she'd put Mark's case, and her own travel bag, away inconspicuously and leaned across to wake him up.

'That was a good night, we really went for it, are you okay?'

Mark sat up abruptly and soon oriented himself. It had always surprised him that he never had much trouble getting up. Probably his time in prison made that inevitable: the morning roll-call hadn't allowed any time for luxuriating in bed.

'Wow, yes, that was great, you were great, we were great from what I can remember. Mind you, I could do with some water pretty quickly, think I rather overdid it.'

Gemma could see that he really had no idea. That would make it easier to keep his fantasy going.

'Let's go down to the breakfast bar and get an early start, may as well make the most of our last day, we can catch the first tender across to the city. It's strange to think that we'll be back home tonight, or early tomorrow at least. And by the way I read somewhere that a decent cooked breakfast is the best cure for any sort of hangover.'

Their flight was scheduled to leave just after 10 that evening and it was only a couple of hours or so back to Gatwick.

She gave Mark a quick kiss, decided to give a final bit of pointless sex with him a miss, and hurried him into his clothes. She didn't want to give him time to check his luggage before they set off for the day.

'We can go across to Lokrum and still get back to the ship early afternoon, in good time to collect our stuff and head to the airport – I found out there's a few of us getting the same flight so we can sort out sharing taxis later.'

It was essential Mark didn't take or even check his suitcase before they left the Uganda for Dubrovnik and then the trip to Lokrum. She left her own case as well, now with her money safely stashed away in it, and just grabbed a small shoulder bag; she told him she could take anything he needed for the morning with her. Although she didn't like leaving the money there, it would look odd carrying a suitcase on their brief excursion to the island. Anyway, it would be safe enough locked in their cabin.

Gemma knew she had to get rid of the money before they left Dubrovnik later; it shouldn't be too much of a problem depositing it at the post office and hopefully sorting a transfer to her account back home. Maybe she'd pop into the post office before they got the ferry to Lokrum and check out what she could do; then return later in the day on the way to the airport with the cash. She'd think of some excuse to do a bit of shopping or something after they docked at the old city and before heading over to Lokrum; probably leave Mark in a café for half an hour or so. At the moment she reckoned she could get him to do just about anything. He was even giving the impression that he thought he'd won her back – bloody idiot, and bloody typical of him, she thought. For now it was important to keep focused on what Mark had actually done; in due course he needed to know she had sussed him out and he hadn't got away with it.

**

After a quick breakfast, they managed to get the first taxi boat of the day, along with a few of the Uganda's crew who generally went to whatever port they were visiting early in the day to stock up on provisions for the next stage of the cruise. The majority of the passengers usually tended to take a leisurely, and typically pretty heavy, breakfast and leave the ship mid-morning. As it was, they docked at the old port just after nine, with the city itself coming to life and preparing for the day ahead. Miguel, the Spanish chef, helped Gemma up on to the quayside with an appreciative glance at her tight jeans. It was never too early in the day for him to flirt.

'I'm going to miss your smile, you know. It's so nice to have some young people on the boat, and some pretty ones too. Have a good day.'

Gemma gave him a quick hug, she couldn't help feeling she would and that things would work out.

'I reckon I will, Miguel. You take care too.'

She grabbed Mark's hand and headed to one of the little quayside cafes, more a kiosk than café really but with a couple of chairs set next to a small metal table at the front.

'Look Mark why don't you get yourself a coffee or something, I've got a little last-minute shopping, souvenirs for a couple of friends, I'll only be half an hour at most then we'll get the ferry across to the island.'

***

As the ferry pulled out from the harbour and headed for the island, Gemma settled back to run things over in her mind. Fortunately the money hadn't proved to be too much of a problem. The counter clerk at the post office didn't seem fazed by her asking if she could deposit and

193

then transfer the cash; it would be open until six o'clock as well, which would give her plenty of time to get back to the ship again to collect her bags and the money. The clerk assured her that it might even be in her account when she got back home. Surprisingly it had all seemed a good deal more straightforward and civilised than she imagined it would have been in England.

There weren't many on their particular ferry to Lokrum. An elderly couple, dressed in matching khaki, explorer-type outfits, two single men both equipped with binoculars, presumably planning to examine some particular inhabitants or species found on the island and a youngish lad who seemed to know the crew and might just have been along for the boat trip. It was November, of course, and although bright was also quite cold. They were on the Skala, which along with the Zrinski was one of the two city-owned boats that made the regular trips between the port and Lokrum. Both it and its crew of two weather-beaten, and presumably local, men looked as if they'd been doing the journey for years. As it motored through the channel between their cruise ship and the nearside shore of Lokrum, Gemma snuggled up to Mark. No harm in keeping him unaware and occupied. She could see he was contented and wondered for a fleeting moment whether perhaps he had changed his mind, and even if she might have somehow got it wrong. He'd even told her over breakfast that last night had made him realise how much he wanted her back. Anyway, that was his look out. She put the thought out of her mind: he'd tried to rip her off, there was no way she wanted him and, even if she had, she'd never have trusted him again. Once a manipulative bastard always one, she figured.

They moored at the little jetty toward the south end of the island. The small snack bar gave the appearance of being open, the tables and chairs were set out for business although there was no one around, and no sign of any waiter. Gemma suggested they walk up to the middle of the island where the now deserted monastery was and then over to Lokrum's own little Dead Sea. They had been told it was a natural and quite deep salt-filled lake that was easy enough to swim in.

'I love swimming but it's probably too cold to do that today, still we can have a look and then get something to eat when we come back, if anyone actually appears to serve us.'

She found her thought processes going into overdrive when Mark replied that he had never really liked or been any good at swimming anyway.

They set off on the well-marked path to the former Benedictine monastery. There had only been the one ferry trip so far that morning and as Gemma and Mark headed out across the island it felt as if they were the only ones there; the silence was quite eerie, almost palpable. The path wound up through a mass of shrubbery and small trees that had mostly lost their foliage. At this time of year, the deserted monastery could be seen from a few hundred yards away; no doubt in the spring and summer it would have been quite hidden until actually stumbled upon. They walked through the cloisters, which unlike most of the monastery had remained pretty much unchanged, and had a quick look at the overgrown gardens and courtyard before following a helpfully positioned if slightly decrepit signpost to Mrtove More, the local name for the Dead Sea.

It only took a few more minutes to reach. As it came into view they were both taken aback: it was a stunning sight even on a chilly autumnal day, and it just didn't seem to fit the rest of the island. It resembled, almost, a mini resort but carved out of the ground. There was a small sort of beach area near where the path had ended and some flat rocks to each side but the sea itself was still and very dark. Across from the would-be beach, and on the other side of the lake, there were steep rocks forming a small cliff, probably little more than thirty yards away, with the water lapping gently against them. It was a clear, bright day and they could make out the Adriatic Sea beyond the far side of the island itself. It would have been the ideal place to while away a summer's day.

'Wow, this is pretty smart.'

Gemma flinched, why did Mark have to adopt some kind of American lilt for no obvious reason? It was time to confront him. She knew she couldn't keep things bottled up much longer.

'Let's wander round to the other side, it looks like we'll get a good view from over there; apparently the water's so deep that people can dive off those rocks in the summer.'

Gemma wasn't certain why she had suggested that, they certainly weren't planning to go swimming. It just seemed like the right place to sort things out. In any case Mark seemed happy enough to let her take the lead.

'Sure, it's lovely here, not that I'm planning any swimming; like I said, it's not really my thing anyway.'

Once they had scrambled round to the rocks overhanging the far side of the lake, Gemma launched into it.

'Listen Mark, do you think I'm some kind of bloody idiot? I know that you've ripped me off, you bastard, and obviously have no intention of coming back to England tonight or even at all. Just what the fuck do you think you're playing at?'

She hadn't said she had already found and taken the money; that could come later. She could see his shock at first and then, almost immediately and if she hadn't known him better almost imperceptibly, his desperate search for an excuse.'

'What do you mean? I'd do anything to stay with you Gemma, you know that. I thought we might work things out between us. It's been great these last few days.'

'Look Mark, stop clutching at straws, I've checked the bank accounts, you've taken something like fifty thousand pounds from our account, if not more, and presumably brought it with you to start some kind of new life or God knows what. But whatever the hell it is, you've certainly ripped me off; and don't come up with some pathetic sort of denial, you're the only one who could have withdrawn that money, and in any case the bank told me it was you.'

She wanted to keep him guessing; and to see him try to squirm his way out of things. She could almost feel his brain grinding into damage limitation mode.

'Okay Gemma, yes I did withdraw that money, but only because I deserved it and if you were going to ditch me I wanted to make sure I wasn't left with nothing. And anyway, I haven't done anything with it, I promise, in fact now we're getting on I really want us to stay together and give things another go. I'd never actually take it if we had a chance of staying together. I love you, you know.'

Even though Gemma knew she was one step ahead, she was finding it difficult to stay calm and control her anger. She folded he arms to stop herself trembling and looked him in the eye.

'So where is the money then, Mark?'

'Well I've just stashed it away at home so we can talk things through when we get back.'

That was it, so much for his sudden pretence of decency and honesty – qualities which were obviously beyond him. She couldn't keep the charade going any longer.

'No way Mark, you're a fucking liar, you better give me that money back now; and if you mess around I'll grass you up about Anne's murder, you know I could, there's nothing to pin anything on me except your word. I'll bloody ruin you, again, you arrogant bastard.'

Mark was disconcerted and rattled, his panic fighting a desperation to come up with a plausible explanation.

'What do you mean give it back now? I haven't got it here, have I? And as I said I bloody deserve it for all I've done for you.'

It was clear Mark was going to hang in there with his excuses. Enough was enough.

'Okay Mark, let's stop messing around. I know exactly what you've done. I've already taken the money from the lining of your stupid enormous suitcase and transferred it all back to an account in my name only. It didn't have to be like this, you know; I actually used to quite like you. Anyway I'm going back to Dubrovnik, you can get back yourself and then you can go where the fuck you like.'

By the time she had finished it was pretty clear that Mark hadn't really been listening; his whole demeanour was changing. He grabbed her. He managed to look both white and livid at the same time. His words were almost spat out.

'But what about last night? I thought we had something. And yes, sure I did take the money but that was before this and over the last few days I've hoped we could get back together and that'd be far more important to me. You've got to believe me. It was only a last resort.'

Things weren't going quite as Gemma had envisaged. Mark looked more than a little manic and clearly unpredictable; she realised that she needed to keep things together for now.

'Mark, last night was a sham, I got you drunk just so as to get my money back. You can't think I want you in my life anymore, we're over. Yes, we might have had some good times but that's finished, we agreed. This was a goodbye trip, you bloody promised.'

She felt his grip tightening around her shoulders and pushed him away. It didn't make a difference. Gemma felt a surge of fear, she hadn't thought about any physical threat. Mark's face was contorted with anger and his fingers dug into the bottom of her neck.

'I can't lose you and you don't want me.'

Mark was plainly desperate and she wasn't in a position to do much. She needed to calm him down pretty quickly or things could go badly wrong.

'Maybe Mark, maybe we could. I do still feel something for you. You know that.'

She looked up at him and smiled, he loosened his hold a little. She knew she had to get away from him. She pushed him with all her strength, kicking out at his shins at the same time. He rocked back and toward the edge of the cliff but had kept enough of a grip on her to drag her with him. She kicked again and this time he lost his balance. He stumbled backwards but still with sufficient of a hold on one of her arms to bring her with him. Time stood still as they fell the few yards to the surface of the lake. As they hit the water they separated; she remembered thinking how cold it was, and how surprisingly dark, before her head hit a ledge jutting out from the rocky cliff wall below the water line.

EPILOGUE

Saturday 13 August 1983 – 5.00 pm

Jeremy was standing on the balcony overlooking the stretch of water between the apartment he was renting up the hill from the old town of Dubrovnik and the little island of Lokrum, which was looking green and lush in spite of the hot summer it had so far endured. It was quite appropriate that Paul Young's 'Wherever I Lay my Hat' was playing in the background on the surprisingly up-to-date local radio station. This had been Jeremy's home for the last few months even though he didn't favour wearing hats much. He stroked his beard, as usual wondering if he'd ever feel comfortable enough to get rid of it. Even though he'd been back in Dubrovnik since early summer, today had been the first time he'd ventured across to the island. It was something he just felt he had to do and today had felt the right time to. However it had been an oddly disturbing experience that he was having difficulty coming to terms with.

Adrijana came through from the kitchen area with a cup of coffee.

'Do you fancy a cup before you have to go down to the restaurant?'

She put her arms round him and kissed the back of his neck.

'Are you okay? You seemed to be miles away. It looks like a storm's on the way; you better get going soon if you don't want to get soaked. They can be pretty dramatic, you know.'

'Hey that's enough questions. I'm fine and no, I won't have a coffee now, I'll get a drink when I get there.'

Jeremy had been working with Howard since returning to the city after a few months in hiding, in Athens for a few weeks before renting a room above a bar in the small town of Malia on the northern coast of Crete. He'd taken enough of the money he'd regained from Gemma to get by, leaving most of it for Howard to invest in expanding the café. And things had gone pretty well by all accounts; as well as the café downstairs, Howard had used the extra money to buy upstairs and open what was beginning to establish itself as a pretty decent upmarket restaurant.

Looking back, meeting Howard had been a godsend. He'd helped Jeremy change his identity and get away from the city without passing any judgement; in fact, he had seemed to be in his element helping arrange things back in November. Even though they'd only re-established contact a few days previously, Jeremy had been happy to trust him with over £40,000 while he laid low. In reality he hadn't had much choice: his options were limited and carrying that amount of cash around wasn't really one of them. Nonetheless his instincts had proved right as far as Howard was concerned. He even quite liked the sound of his new name too.

He grabbed a coat and gave Adrijana a quick kiss.

'You going to come down before closing, have a quick drink maybe?'

'Yes probably, will pop in on my mum and dad on the way down, see you later.'

It was just after five o'clock and it would take him about 15 minutes to walk down the hill to the old city and the restaurant. Although still hot, it was a pleasant enough walk, onto Ulica Franca Supila and then down past the Hotel Excelsior, originally built seventy odd years ago but regularly upgraded to maintain its position as the most elegant and best situated place for the rich and famous to stay – after all, both Elizabeth Taylor and Queen Elizabeth II had been guests, so it had some credibility. As he had expected, the pebbled beach outside the city gates was still pretty packed at this time of day – tourism really was beginning to take off in Dubrovnik, and so much the better, thought Jeremy. Howard's Taverna was just off Placa Ulica, the main thoroughfare running through the old city. In spite of its lack of originality, Jeremy was happy enough with the name, he wasn't after any publicity and it was Howard's venture after all. When he arrived it would be the transition period between the daytime café trade and the arrival of the early evening diners. The general arrangement was for Jeremy to oversee the evening business with Howard doing the daytime shift. Most evenings, though, Howard and Branka would come and join Jeremy and Adrijana for a few drinks and to sort out any of the practical issues that came with the business. Howard had an apartment just a few minutes away in the old city itself. Branka's friend Adrijana had been a regular visitor when Jeremy had returned to the city and it had been a stroke of luck that she was good looking and single. After one of their post-closing drinking sessions, Jeremy and she had carried on and gone on into the town before ending up at the apartment Howard had sorted for Jeremy's return after they had decided he'd be better off away from the city for a few months at least.

Apparently Yugoslavian women were renowned for their beauty and Adrijana gave credence to that; tall and slender, she had a Mediterranean complexion, with olive coloured skin, light brown hair and deep brown eyes. Although she usually tended to dress casually in sandals, T-shirts and skirts, she managed to radiate both elegance and sexiness. Jeremy felt as happy as he had done for years. Howard himself had proved to be easy to work with and good company. He had become something of an expert in the local liqueurs and Jeremy had quickly learned to appreciate them himself. He had soon developed a taste for Rakia, or Grappa as the regulars called it, some of which was well over fifty per cent alcohol; but even more so for Slivovitz, made from damson plums and typically served from elegant, leather-wrapped bottles. He certainly hadn't missed the drugs which he reckoned paled by comparison.

As he reached Ploce Gate, the Eastern entrance to the old city, the sun was still shining although the storm clouds they'd seen from the balcony were gathering force. A cruise ship was just visible on the horizon, no doubt heading for the port for a weekend stopover. It seemed, to the outside world at least, that things hadn't changed that much since the fateful day last November. He'd actually been back to the scene that lunchtime and while being strangely moved by it, it was apparent that those events hadn't impacted on the wider world. It had

204

been the first time since then and the first time under his new guise as Jeremy. He had needed to see for himself whether the scene matched his memory, and the occasional nightmares too.

As it had turned out, the island of Lokrum was becoming ever more popular with tourists, while Mrtvo More itself had looked quite benign and inviting, even. There was no sign of the accident nine months previously; certainly none of the bathers there showed any concern. The only acknowledgement of Gemma's death seemed to be a sign that hadn't been there last November warning of the dangers of jumping off the rocks. It didn't appear to be having much effect and Jeremy hadn't been able to take his eyes off the show-offs diving from the rocks without a care for the danger.

That day last November, when he was still Mark, remained etched on his mind. As they hit the water Mark had assumed that was it; one hand was grasping Gemma's arm but they separated as they sank. She had been nearest to the rocky wall and he heard her head crack against a protruding stone. He had managed to grab some kind of bush or plant and had eventually scrambled to the surface and hauled himself up to the platform they'd fallen off. There had been no sign of Gemma.

It hadn't taken him long to realise that there was no way he could save Gemma; or that if he reported this it wouldn't look good for him. And it hadn't taken him too much longer to realise that the money he'd taken back in England and brought with him on the cruise must still be in Gemma's things on the Uganda; and that his best bet would be to get back and away as soon as he could.

Sure, it had been an accident but he wasn't prepared to risk trying to convince the police or anyone else of that. It wasn't as if he had wished any of this on Gemma, or that he could help her now – of course he would have done if there had been any chance of saving her. The tragedy was that in the end he had changed his mind about harming her and would have been quite happy to have left her to go back to England and stayed on in Dubrovnik alone to develop the venture with Howard. If she hadn't gone off on one and threatened to grass him up over the death of her mother, which she had engineered anyway, then none of this would have happened. As usual, it hadn't really been his fault – why hadn't she let him explain? It had helped his state of mind that he knew it had been an accident, but he also knew it would be highly unlikely to be seen as such.

As it was, he had tried to wring out his jeans and jacket with little effect and had headed back to the jetty and café; it had been as deserted as before and he managed to take some kind of overcoat and scarf from a rack at the back of the café which covered most of his other clothes. It was a stroke of luck that it was the Zrinski, the other of the two ferries, that had appeared after a few minutes, with its crew having no idea that he had arrived on the island with a woman. He'd got back to Dubrovnik and then the cruise ship without attracting any particular attention. Sure enough the money he had originally taken was now stored neatly at the bottom of Gemma's case. No one had raised even an eyebrow when he'd left the ship with his and her suitcases, telling the crew members he came across that he was meeting Gemma in the city ready for the flight back to England. There had been a slight panic when he had tried to surreptitiously dump her luggage into the harbour; the noise when it hit the water seemed to drown everything else out, but no one else showed any sign of noticing.

He had headed up to Howard's café with no particular plan in mind although he realised he would need some help and that Howard was his only option. As it turned out, Howard had been amazing; he agreed it wouldn't look good for Mark and offered to help him hide. He turned out to have more about him than Mark had realised, and had managed to organise getting a false identity and passport from some contact he had in the city. They decided it would be best for Mark to leave the city for a few months at least and Howard promised to keep an eye on things and see if he could pick up if anything was reported about Gemma. Mark was happy enough to pay him for the identity change and then to leave the bulk of his money to invest in the café – after all, that had been on his mind even before the accident with Gemma. Also it might not have been too sensible to go into hiding with a large stash of money and it certainly wouldn't be sensible to try and deposit it anywhere officially. Although he was the first to admit he wasn't the best judge of character, Mark had just felt there was something genuine about Howard. They agreed that after a few months and before the summer season, Mark could come back under his new identity and work with Howard in some kind of partnership. As Howard had said, there was no reason for anyone to connect Mark with him. They had agreed that the best thing for the moment would be to hide at Howard's for a few days while a passport was sorted out and then to get away as soon as possible. As it turned out that had taken a few days and Mark had arrived in Athens as Jeremy before the end of November.

Saturday 13 August 1983 – 11.30 pm

Adrijana poured herself a drink and sat next to him.

'How was it tonight?'

'Yes, busy, pretty packed between 9 and 10.'

'Great. Look, leave the tidying, let's go back and have a nightcap at home. I've got some good news: my dad said he'd buy the apartment for me, apparently he knows the owner is keen to sell it. You know, I think he likes you and I reckon it's also because he wants me to stay here in Dubrovnik, close to the family. And after all he can well afford it.'

So things hadn't gone too badly. He was sorry about Gemma but then it was an accident; and who knows, perhaps fate?